BADA-BING, BADA-TOMB!

THE DAVE BEAUCHAMP SERIES

Kill the Mother!
Eats to Die For!
Dead and in Person!
Bada-Bing, Bada-Tomb!

ALSO BY MICHAEL MALLORY

The Mural: A Novel of Horror

BADA-BING, BADA-TOMB!

MICHAEL MALLORY

A Dave Beauchamp Mystery

WILDSIDE PRESS

Published by Wildside Press LLC.
wildsidepress.com | bcmystery.com

ONE

As soon as I opened my apartment door, I sensed I was in trouble.

She stood there looking at me accusingly like I had done something that totally upended her life. Maybe I had, but if so I couldn't remember what.

"Are you going to let me in?" she demanded in a vocal register that women normally get from a lifetime of cigarette smoking, though as long as I've known her she's never smoked.

And I've known her all my life.

"Come on in, Mom," I said.

Once she was inside my apartment with the door safely closed she gave me a perfunctory hug. Mom had always been leery of any display of affection in public. Sometimes that extended to private.

Pamela Beauchamp was only about five-feet-four, a good seven inches shorter than me. At fifty-nine she was enviably slender (at least according to my former girlfriend who was soon frightened away by her) and had a mostly-unlined face. Nature had served her well (*It had better*, I could imagine her saying), though her one concession to vanity was keeping her hair dyed a reddish-brown without the slightest trace of gray.

She was in no way a threatening-looking person.

But I'd hate to go up against her in a knife-fight.

Mom crossed to the beat-up sofa in the living room and sat down.

"Well, aren't you going to offer your mother anything?" she asked.

"Oh, sorry. Can I get you some coffee? Tea? Soda?"

"No, I'm fine. But you should always ask first, and not make your guest beg for it. Sometimes I think I'm the only one in this family with any sense of manners."

A woman after my own heart! a voice said inside my head. It was Bette Davis, one of the many Golden Age Hollywood stars who weigh in from time inside my cranium. I know it sounds insane—at the very least schizophrenic—but I've learned to live with it. Sometimes it's a good deal, as when the voices offer support, or even wisdom that prods me into thinking.

Other times they delight in kicking me when I'm already down.

Deep down inside I know they're all me, even the ones wearing steel-toed boots. At least they're all coming *from* me on some level, a manifestation of the fact that I've been a film buff for my entire life. But in a way they are also comforting. I have come to depend on the kindness of old dead movie stars. Even so, I don't broadcast that fact to anyone else. Mom knew nothing about the Hollywood Victory Caravan inside my head, and I had no intention now of reloading her rifle with bullet-shaped, secret idiosyncrasies.

"All right, Mom," I said, plunking down in my sagging armchair, "to what do I owe this pleasure?"

"Well, far be it from me to interfere with your life," she began, "but I've been meaning to talk to you about this thing you do for quite some time."

"You mean private investigation?"

"I mean nearly getting yourself killed. I read in the newspaper that you were held at gunpoint by a crazy woman."

"A famous crazy woman."

"What difference does that make?"

"It shows that I know a higher class of murderers."

"You seem to find this amusing."

"Being held at gunpoint? No, I don't find it amusing at all. But it can be part of the job."

"Then get another job. Being a private detective is not a normal way to make a living."

I had to admit that was true. But all most people know of investigation work is what they see on television: car chases, fist fights, one-night stands, and an all's-well-that-ends-well freeze frame over the closing credits. Real life PI work was a lot duller. But having been dumped by the large law firm which had employed me and finding that no other firm seemed interested in taking me on, it was a way to earn money. Skip-tracing lost pets, photographing perpetrators of insurance fraud, or simply just finding people who had fallen out of touch with their families were the backbones of my work—though I had indeed been involved in a few high-profile murder cases.

Those were not by choice.

"Mom, if it makes you feel better, I'm seriously thinking of closing my office," I offered, "at least after the conclusion of my current case."

"Are you going to get shot at again?"

"Not this time."

The case in question involved Vince Mazetta, a pet food magnate who looked and acted like a Central Casting Mafioso from a 1950s gangster movie. He phoned me a few days back claiming someone was out to get him, and that he'd received a classic threatening letter comprised of words clipped from a newspaper. Even though it sounded more like a television plot than a real threat, I agreed to look into it since I owed him a favor.

The thought, however, that he might simply be pranking me as revenge for a pretense of mine that he'd swallowed hook, line, and sinker a month or so back, was not off the table.

Mom took my announcement with surprise. "Really?" she asked. "What will you do, then?"

"I don't know. Maybe get a job as an usher in a movie theatre."

"Oh, yes, of course, you and your dopey movies. You know your father could have gotten you hired at his firm."

That was likely true. My father was a successful senior attorney at the prestigious Century City firm of Allen, Garbedian and Lomax LLC, and he probably could have brought me in, where I would spend my days enduring the scorn of everyone for being employed simply because I was Carl's kid. "I didn't want to trade on Dad's reputation and standing, okay?"

"So you're also probably going to tell me that you don't care that he's had a heart attack."

"*What*?" I yelled. "Good god, why didn't you say that when you first came in? Is he all right?"

"He's fine, it wasn't a large one. I didn't say anything at first because I know you. I knew you'd over-react."

I took a deep breath. If the situation was dire, I doubted even my mom would be this cavalier about it. "Is he in the hospital?" I asked.

"He went in last night and they kept him overnight for observation. I'm told that as heart attacks go it was not very serious, but he is going to have to slow down. So here I am."

"I'm not following you."

"You need to come back and work for him at his firm, take some of the pressure off of him. Since, as you say, you're quitting this private eye nonsense anyway, there's no reason not to."

I could think of a few.

It's not like I had anything against my dad...quite the opposite, in fact. Carl Beauchamp was a world-class movie buff, which is how I inherited the mania. We could talk film for hours. He was also a fine and patient father. But there was a big difference between us professionally. Dad was a terrific lawyer, one who regularly appeared on the "Best Lawyers in the City" lists in *Los Angeles Magazine*. My signature moment as an attorney was getting canned.

"Mom, you know I'm not a very good lawyer," I said.

She rolled her eyes dramatically. "You passed the bar, didn't you? Why would they have let you do that if you weren't a good lawyer? Where did you go to learn how to sell yourself short, anyway?"

There's no place like home, Judy Garland's voice said inside my head.

"What hospital is he in?" I asked, hoping to change the subject.

"Cedars, but there's no sense in going there because, like I said, he'll be back home tomorrow."

"Can I at least call?"

"That would be a good idea. Then you two can talk about your coming into the firm."

"I didn't say I would, Mom."

"Well, whatever. It's only your father's life at stake."

I used to worry about offending my mother every time I threw my arms up in the air and sighed in frustration, but not anymore. Maybe that's the difference between being seventeen and thirty-three.

However, this time she seemed to be aware that she was pushing my buttons harder and faster than Liberace pounding the keys for *Flight of the Bumblebee*, and uncharacteristically backed off.

"How long will this case you're on take?"

"Probably not too long," I said. The truth was I had only just started. Vince Mazetta had given me a list of "goombahs" who might want him out of the way, but even he couldn't come up with a reason why. I tried running the names through a database and not one popped up, which could mean they were modern mobsters who knew how to keep their personal information from sliding onto a database.

Or it could mean he was yanking my chain.

The front door opened again, and this time it was Hannah, toting two reusable plastic shopping bags overflowing with groceries. "Hi, Dave," she said, setting the bags down in order to close the door behind her. "They had a special on boneless chicken breasts, so I…oh, I didn't know someone was coming over tonight."

"Neither did I," I said. "Hannah, this is my mom, Pamela Beauchamp."

"Your mom!" Hannah squealed running over to her, sitting down beside her, and wrapping her arms around her. "I'm Hannah Skaal. I guess you've heard about me."

"No, I haven't," Mom replied, coolly.

"Really? Dave, we're going to be married and you haven't even told your mother?"

"You're going to be *what*?" Mom shouted.

Just kill yourself now, kid, Humphrey Bogart said inside my head.

"Of course I was going to tell you, Mom, but I wanted to wait until… well, until we were in a new place."

"What new place?" Mom asked.

"We've been looking around," Hannah said. "Now that we have money."

"What money?"

"We're coming into an inheritance."

"Inheritance!" Mom snapped. "Aren't you getting a little ahead of yourself? After all, your father is in the hospital one night for observation!"

"I'm not talking about Dad. I'm talking about Palmer Hanley."

Both Hannah and I had been remembered quite generously in the will of the recently deceased Palmer Hanley, whom Hannah had nursed for a number of years while both were held as virtual prisoners by a pseudo-religious cult. I had managed to rescue them both during the course of one of those high-profile murder cases. As a result I became an heir to the old fellow's estate, which was extensive. Hannah's and my inheritances combined ran to nearly two million

"Your dad's in the hospital, Dave?" Hannah asked.

"Yes, but according to Mom he's doing well."

Mom, meanwhile, had her thinking face on. "Palmer Hanley," she said, "oh, the old conman who started that dopey religion."

"There's more to it than that," I said quickly, before Hannah had a chance to react. "He wasn't the crook, others were in his name. Hannah was very close to him and I became so, and he remembered us."

"That's him over there," Hannah said, pointing to the ceramic urn sitting on a small, round table, which contained Palmer's mortal remains.

"You're joking," my mother said.

"Nope, that's him, all right," I said. "He'll be moving with us."

"Good lord."

In an attempt to change back to the original subject, I said, "So anyway, we're going to need a place with a little more room."

"Because there's three of you now?"

"Well, he will be the one paying the bills," I replied.

"Oh, you're such a rotten kid," Mom muttered, which caused Hannah to frown until she noticed me grinning and realized this was a very old routine.

"Hannah and I are looking at houses," I went on. "The truth is I'm not going to miss this apartment all that much. It's served its purpose but it's time to move on. Besides, people have a bad habit of showing up here unannounced."

"Well, I like that!" my mother bristled.

"I didn't mean you, Mom."

"I'll go put the groceries away," Hannah said, rushing to retrieve the bags on the floor by the door, and then practically running them into our small kitchen.

Attempting to dig my way out of the grave faster than Andrée Melly in *Brides of Dracula*, I blundered on. "What I meant was that some people, who were involved in my last case, took it upon themselves to come over here instead of going to my office like I'd prefer. You remember all those people coming over, right, hon?"

"You mean that horrible Miranda Love, who threw up on the rug?" Hannah responded.

The memory of that visit by Miranda Love, a former movie star now reduced to selling her signature at celebrity shows, still haunted my sleep.

"And not just Miranda," I said. "Others have found out where I live and appeared at the door, wanting things from me. So if we move, and don't tell anyone where our new place is, people won't suddenly show up without warning."

"Like me," Mom sniffed.

Bogie, you're right, I thought. *Hand me the cyanide.*

Hannah, bless her, broke the agonizingly long silence that followed by saying, "If you need to go see your dad, Dave, I can hold up dinner."

"Visiting hours have already ended," Mom said. "Coming by the house tomorrow would be good, I think."

"Can I come, too?" Hannah asked. "I'd love to meet your dad."

"Sure," I said. "Would you like to stay for dinner, Mom? Do we have enough, Hannah?"

"Oh, I'm sure we do," she said. "How about it, Mrs. Beauchamp?"

My mother got up from the sofa and went to the tiny kitchen. "Thank you so much for the offer," she said, "but I'll take a rain-check. And if I'm really gaining a daughter, you are not allowed to call me Mrs. Beauchamp. I am either Pamela or Mom."

"How about Ma Beauchamp," Hannah asked.

Mom actually smiled.

Boy, howdy.

"Your father should be home after lunch," the newly-dubbed Ma Beauchamp said, walking toward the door. "Any time in the afternoon would be fine."

"We'll be there," I said. "Do you want me to call first?"

"Oh, no, don't do that. I'd hate for you to ruin your reputation as the king of surprises. I will see you tomorrow."

At the door she gave me another perfunctory hug, using it as opportunity to whisper in my ear, "So, what's the attraction, that red hair or those boobs of hers?"

"It's true love," I whispered back, preventing myself from adding, *you probably wouldn't understand.*

Mom showed herself out.

When she was gone, Hannah said, "Your mother is such a sweet woman."

"My mother is a lot of things, Hannah, but I wouldn't call her 'sweet' to her face if I were you. She doesn't like being thought of as sweet."

"You must be exaggerating."

"I've known her all my life. If you were on the Titanic, Pamela Beauchamp is who you'd want in your lifeboat. If you ever needed something, and needed it badly, like life-or-death badly, she would be there for you. But if you only *want* something, as opposed to *needing* it, then forget it. If you're having a bad day, or week, or year, and you want someone to offer a little bit of sympathy or understanding, well, you're better off going to the family dog."

"Huh," Hannah said.

"But having unloaded all of that baggage onto the floor, I have to admit that she accepted you in a way that surprised me."

"You think so? I hope we can be friends."

"I'm not worried, particularly after seeing her smile in reaction to that 'Ma Beauchamp' business."

Maybe she thought the girl said Ma Barker, Shelley Winters chimed in, unhelpfully.

TWO

The next day we were just about to head out to my parents' house when Vince Mazetta called.

"Beauchamp, I hope you got something to report," he said, "because I got another letter."

"What kind of a letter?" I made the mistake of asking.

After an annoyed exhalation, he hollered, "A letter from the Nobel Foundation saying I've been awarded the prize for cat food! What the hell kind of letter do you *think* I'm talking about?"

"Um, a threatening one?"

"*Yes*, a threatening one! I need you to see it. I'll send Philly to pick you up and bring you here."

I had met Philly once. He could have been an extra in *Planet of the Apes*, without the makeup.

"Actually, Mr. Mazetta, I have something of an emergency I need to take care of right now."

"You don't consider a death threat an emergency?"

I glanced at my watch. "How about giving me a couple hours and then I'll come by your office."

"Jesus. Okay, but at two hours and one second, I send Philly to find you."

He hung up on me.

"Problem?" Hannah asked.

"Vince Mazetta wants to see me in two hours and I don't know how long it will take with Dad."

"So maybe you're a little late. What's Mr. Mazetta going to do to you?"

I really did not want to find out.

It was about 1:15 when we got to my folks' home. Growing up in the Spanish Colonial Revival-style house in Cheviot Hills, on the city's west side, was like living in a mansion. By high school I realized it was one of the smaller houses on the street.

Mom's BMW was parked in the driveway, leaving me to assume Dad's Lexus was in the garage.

"Wow, what a nice house!" Hannah said, getting out of my poor 2001 Corolla that I had vowed to replace once the inheritance from Palmer Hanley came through.

Feeling that ringing the doorbell was too cold and formal I knocked on the door and then tried it to see if it was locked. It wasn't, so I pushed it open and stepped in. "Knock-knock," I called, "it's Dave."

My dad came shuffling out to greet us, a lopsided grin on his face. "Hey, son thanks for coming," he said, extending his hand, which I took.

His grip was weak.

"How are you doing, Dad?"

"Oh, I don't know. I'm still here. Is this Hannah?"

"Hello, Mr. Beauchamp," she said, beaming.

"Please call me Carl," he said. "Come on in, both of you."

Dad was sixty-four but he looked a few years older. He's the opposite of me. People constantly tell me I look like a college kid even though I'm thirty-three. Maybe Dad was my personal picture of Dorian Gray.

On the way to the living room, Dad asked Hannah, "So, do you like old movies?"

"I'm learning to," she said with a smile.

Good answer.

It was only when we were all seated—Dad in his favorite chair and Hannah and I (quite appropriately) on the loveseat—that Mom made an appearance. "Can I get anything for anyone?" she asked in lieu of *hello.*

"I'd love some coffee, Pammy," Dad said.

"You're not supposed to have caffeine, remember?"

Dad sighed. "Ice water then."

Mom looked over at us and I said, "Nothing for me, thanks."

"I'm fine," Hannah said, smiling.

She went back into the kitchen.

"So, Dad, what happened?"

"Oh, I'm sure your mother made more of it than is really there," he replied. "I started having chest pains Monday night and your mom rushed me into emergency, and they decided it was a small heart attack. They kept me until this morning, checking everything out. Complete oil and lube, you know. Then they sent me home with enough pills to make Oscar Levant jealous."

Hannah looked at me quizzically and I whispered, "I'll explain later."

"Now I'm supposed to watch my diet and exercise more, and drop about fifteen pounds. Then I'll be good as new…as long as you're buying a retread."

"How do you feel?" I asked.

"Tired mostly. The pain's gone and one of those pills they gave me for high blood pressure is making me pee like a racehorse."

"It must be a diuretic," Hannah said. "The effects won't last forever."

"Hannah worked as a nurse," I said.

"Hello, nurse!" Dad leered, and then chuckled.

Mom returned with his ice water (which was likely not going to help his bathroom issue).

"I hope you'll be able to explain to your father that there is indeed life beyond the office," she said. "He's being obstinate."

"That's because I have no intention of retiring," Dad stated. "I wouldn't even get my full social security benefits if I quit now."

"You won't get them at all if you're dead."

"Oh, for heaven's sake…look, we don't need to burden the kids with all this."

"We need to explain to Dave his responsibility."

"Responsibility?"

"His responsibility to help you out."

"It's not the boy's fault I had a little ticker episode."

"We sent him to law school. The least he could do is use the education we bought and paid for toward preventing you from working yourself to death."

We're off on the road to a guilt trip, Bob Hope and Bing Crosby harmonized inside my head.

"Okay, look," I began, "if you want me to help Dad out at the law firm, I'll do what I can. But I still have to work on the one investigative case I have going. I can't abandon a client."

"Abandoning your father is all right, though," Mom stabbed.

"Objection, your honor," Dad said, raising a hand and silencing her. Then he turned to me. "I'll be off work for two or three days, minimum, Davy. If you could go into the office and pick up some files from cases I've got going and bring them back here, that would be a big help right there."

"I can do that."

"See? How hard was that?" Mom said, triumphantly.

Round one goes to the Maternal Mauler! the voice of Bill Baldwin ring-announced in my mind. Okay, you don't know the name, but you've seen him a hundred times in films and on TV, often playing a sports announcer.

"Could I use the bathroom?" Hannah asked, and Mom offered to show her where it was.

Once they were both gone, Dad leaned forward, exerting a level of effort that made me worry. "You need to cut your mother a little slack, Davy," he said. "She's been worried sick since they took me into the hospital. She's still on edge."

"All I said was I'd try to help."

"I know, I know. But you were thinking something else. I can always tell when you're thinking something. You get this distracted look on your face, almost like you're listening to another a voice no one else can hear."

A hit, a palpable hit! the voice of Peter Cushing as Osric said inside my head.

"You did it again just now," Dad said.

"Dad…are there any bats in our ancestral belfry?"

He laughed and said, "What the hell kind of question is that?"

"I'm curious is all."

"Bats? A couple old ones, maybe, but none flying over the cuckoo's nest that I know of. Why? You want to make sure you don't pass anything on to your kids?"

"Um, I hadn't really thought about it."

"Well, now that you've got a girl, you will at some point. You've done pretty damn well, too. She's really got a rack on her."

If I frowned, Dad didn't notice. His earlier "Hello, nurse" crack was understandable, since it was an old vaudeville reference. But crass sexual remarks about women were simply not like him. I wondered about his medication.

"Speaking of Hannah," he continued, "I hope she's done in the bathroom because I have to pee again, and I don't want to drag my butt upstairs."

At that moment she walked back into the living room.

"Oh, good," Dad said, struggling out of the chair. I stood ready to help him at any moment, but I sensed he didn't want help. "Everything come out all right, honey?" he cracked as he shuffled past.

"I guess so," Hannah replied, looking a little nonplussed.

When Dad was out of sight I whispered, "Whatever he's taking seems to be playing with his mind a little bit. He's normally not into vulgar remarks."

"Maybe I should look at what they've prescribed and make sure they're compatible," she whispered back.

"That's a good idea, but you'll have to do it without Mom knowing. I'll tell you what. I'll go into the kitchen with her and keep her occupied while you sneak upstairs into their bedroom. Top of the stairs, turn left, first door. My guess is Dad keeps his pill bottles on the dresser."

"What if I get caught?"

"I'll make excuses."

She dashed quietly up the stairs, which was easy since the stairway, like the rest of the house, still wore thick 1970s carpeting that muffled footfalls.

I went to the kitchen. Mom was standing in front of the sink, rinsing out glasses.

"It's for the best, you know," she said. "Your father's retirement, I mean."

"I know."

Then she turned around and gave me *that look*.

"What's Hannah doing upstairs?" she asked.

I knew better than to deny anything. I don't know how Mom knew, but she knew. She always knew.

"She got something in her eye and asked if we had any eye drops," I lied. "Since Dad's in the bathroom down here, I sent her upstairs to look."

Mom chose not to reply, but turned back to the sink.

A moment later Hannah returned.

"Did you find any eye drops in the bathroom?" I asked, frantically winking at her. Fortunately she finally got the message.

"Oh, no," she replied. "I couldn't find any so I just splashed a little water in my eyes. That seems to have taken care of it."

"You want a wet rag?" Mom asked.

"I'm fine now," Hannah replied.

Then Dad oozed back into the kitchen and said, "Lord, I could learn to hate those pills. Davy, let's go into my office and I'll make you a list of the files I need you to get."

I followed him into the home office, which was far better furnished than my professional one in Sherman Oaks. Seating himself in his leather chair he said, "You know, I haven't asked you how your own career is going. Your mom was a little upset over that business with the gun and the taser."

"Oh, the newspaper reports of my last case were a little exaggerated," I fibbed. In truth I had been held at gun and taser-point by a killer, and only barely escaped with my life. But there was no sense in upsetting my dad further. "There might be less of that sort of thing from now on. I'm about to come into some money through an inheritance."

"That's what your mom said, from the old guy with the cult."

I didn't bother explaining the finer points of Palmer Hanley and the Temple of Theotologics yet again. Instead I said, "What it really means, Dad, is I'll be able to pay back the loan you gave me to open up my office."

"Oh, I'm not worried about that." He reached for a pad of legal paper and a pen and began to write. "I hope you can read this. I've gotten used to dictating and my handwriting's gone to hell." When he was finished he slid the pad over to me. "These are the files I need you to pick up from the office."

"I can make out the first four but not this one," I said. "Clurman?"

"Cleerman," he said, spelling it. "Sexual harassment lawsuit brought by a former employee of his."

"Is he guilty?"

Dad shrugged. "One man's dirty joke is another woman's harassment."

"And you're defending him?"

"That's my job."

"But if he is guilty and you get him off, won't other women suffer from his behavior?"

"I'm not calling future women as witnesses, Davy. Look, anyone is entitled to the strongest defense possible. That's the way it works. If we start arguing against the adversarial system of law, then all of society is going to suffer."

"I was never cut out to be a lawyer," I confessed.

Dad smiled sadly. "I have to agree. You've always seen things in terms of right versus wrong rather than legal versus illegal. That's an admirable trait in a lot of ways and for a lot of professions, but the law isn't one of them. Oh, Christ, don't look at me like that."

"Like what?"

"Like you just saw Atticus Finch coming out of a whorehouse. You always looked up to me like I was some kind of hero, Davy, but I'm not a hero. I'm a lawyer. A damn good lawyer, if I do say so myself, but my feet aren't made of marble. Heroes only exist in the movies. You know that."

"But how can you turn off your sense of justice for the sake of a case?"

"What the hell are you talking about? Justice is the whole point! I've dedicated my life to the law because it's the rare system that actually works. When did you become so self-righteous, anyway? Is that what pretending you're Philip Marlowe does to you?"

"What pretending to be Philip Marlowe has done is shown me some of the worst of human nature. I wasn't prepared for that when I started the job, but it's there. I've seen people do things that are indefensible, even by the best lawyer on the planet."

"Well, fortunately I haven't," he uttered. "Can you get that stuff here by tomorrow?"

"Yes."

"Great. Thanks, son."

"You're welcome. Now button your fly, Atticus, Scout's watching."

After a three count he started chuckling. "Shit," he uttered. "If I were your mother I'd call you a rotten kid."

After Dad laboriously got out of his chair, the two of us left his office and went back into the living room, where we could hear Mom and Hannah in the kitchen, laughing.

"Should I be worried?" I asked.

"I don't know," Dad replied. Then he checked his watch and said, "Christ, it's time for some more damn pills. They're upstairs."

"I can go get them for you if you want."

"I'm not dead yet, Davy."

He dragged himself up the stairs and the "womenfolk" returned from the kitchen.

Say that again, buster, and I'll sock you one in the whistle-hole, Lauren Bacall warned inside my head.

Mom glanced at the paper in my hand.

"This is a list of files Dad wants me to bring from the office," I said. "I'll stop by tomorrow and drop them off."

She nodded. Then Dad appeared at the top of the stairs and called, "As long as I've made it up here, I think I'm going to lie down for a while. I'll see you tomorrow, Davy."

"Right," I called back.

"That's actually good," Mom said. "I've been trying to get him to rest more, but he insists on coming down and puttering around as though nothing's wrong."

"If it's his first heart attack he doesn't have any experience for dealing with it," Hannah reasoned. "He'll learn what he needs to do pretty quickly."

Mom nodded and clutched Hannah's hand for a moment.

Jeez…*affection!*

I looked at my watch; nearly an hour had passed since I'd foolishly agreed to see Vince Mazetta in two hours. What was even more foolish was that I had not figured into the equation time to drop Hannah off back home before going to see him.

Then again since Hannah and Mom were getting along so well, maybe she could stay here until I was finished with Vince.

As it turned out, they were both agreeable to that arrangement. In fact, Mom asked if we wanted to stay for dinner.

"Maybe another time," I said. "I honestly don't know how long this is going to take, and I don't want to keep everybody waiting."

I left shortly after that and, while driving away, tried to focus on what I was going to say to Vince. This wasn't even a paying job, since in classic mob fashion he was calling on me to return a favor. Whatever his background was or wasn't, though, I liked Vince. He was a genuine character in a fabled city that was becoming blander by the year.

Yeah? Tell that to the horses he turns into dog food, Mickey Rooney's voice sneered.

You can't please everyone.

THREE

Cudahy is a small independent city on the southeast edge of Los Angeles, located in the freeway zone. As was the case with my earlier visits, the sky was hazed over like it was waiting to be washed.

But I was not here to sightsee.

The Perfect Friends Pet Food Company was housed in a massive, ugly structure that covered most of a block in an industrial section. The air around it was not fragrant, which was not surprising given what went on behind the gray walls. Despite its assault on any number of the senses, the edifice still contained the most valuable commodity in Los Angeles: a free parking lot. After stashing my Corolla in an open spot, I entered the building and was greeted by the same sardonic receptionist I'd encountered on my first visit here.

"Hello, Mr. Beauchamp," she said, looking as though she was weighing whether a smile was worth the trouble.

"Hello. I'm flattered you remember me."

"Oh, I didn't. I got a note an hour ago that said you were going to show up by two o'clock or else."

It's always nice to make an impression on people.

"I'll let Mr. M know you're here," she said.

The second member of Vince Mazetta's inner circle was a young woman named Marnie who dressed like Kim Novak in *Vertigo*. At least that was her garb the last time I saw her. Today she appeared in the lobby in a very smartly-tailored man's suit and tie. Her blond hair was slicked down, parted, and brushed over her ears.

"Let me guess," I said. "Katharine Hepburn in *Sylvia Scarlett*."

"You're good," Marnie replied with a smile. "Walk this way."

You don't really expect me to fall for that one, do you? the mordant voice of William Powell asked.

Marnie took me to the private office of Vince Mazetta, which now had a very large, uniformed security guard stationed outside.

"Sal, this is Dave Beauchamp," Marnie said. "Mr. M is expecting him."

"Even so," the guard said, holding out his arms as a request for me to do the same. Once he had patted me down and found nothing, he said, "Okay. Can't be too careful, sir."

"I agree," I said.

Vince Mazetta—all five-feet-one of him—was standing behind an enormous oak desk with his back to us. He glanced over at a modern-design floor clock which that moment chimed two, and then turned around. "Right on time," he said, "I like that."

Mazetta made no attempt to shake my hand. He simply directed me into a chair and dismissed Marnie, who turned and left without another word.

"Okay, Beauchamp, what have you got for me?" Vince asked.

"Well, nothing really. I've tried to check out those names you gave me, and I can't find them."

"Oh, that's great, that's just swell. That's dandy. Someone's trying to kill me, and you can't find anybody. Here, look at this."

He slid a letter across his desk. It resembled a classic movie-style threatening note except that instead of its words cut from magazines and pasted onto the page, someone had used a computer to create and print a mélange of different type styles, fonts, sizes, and colors to form letters. Some words had their own individual background colors to resemble an actual clipping.

It read: *You better take this seriously. You don't have much time left. Your days are 3, 4, 5, 6, 7, 8, 9…*

It took me a couple seconds to figure out the last part meant *Your days are numbered.*

"Well?" Mazetta said.

"How did you get this?" I asked.

"It was in an envelope that'd been tucked under the windshield wiper of my car."

"While it was parked?"

He gave that sigh again, then shouted, "No, the guy ran down the street beside us while Philly was driving and stuck it there when he wasn't looking! *Of course* it was while the car was parked!"

"Um, sorry. So this is your limo we're talking about?"

"Yeah, the limo. I stopped driving myself years ago except for…"

"Except for what?"

"Sometimes I just need to get away from everything and everybody," he said. "I have a little beach house around Zuma and a '68 Mustang in cherry condition. That I drive myself. But this time it was the limo."

"Where was it parked?"

"At Cyril Gore's in Brentwood. You know what Cyril Gore's is?"

I nodded. While I couldn't afford the clothes there (yet), I knew that Cyril Gore's was the clothier to the stars—male stars, exclusively—beginning in the 1950s and continuing to this day. Cyril himself is long gone but his family has continued to operate the store. I'd bet that Mazetta's suits contained any number of invisible tailoring tricks which collectively gave the illusion of his being taller. "Do you go to Cyril Gore's often?" I asked.

"I'm a regular customer, but I don't live there," he said. "Once every couple months, maybe."

"Do you make an appointment?"

"I don't have to. Why?"

"Because if nobody knew you were coming, it would imply you were being followed."

"Followed?"

"How else would someone know you were going to be at the store on that day at that time in order to put the letter on your windshield? Unless…"

"Spit it out, Beauchamp."

"Did anyone else know you were going to Cyril Gore's?"

"My wife knew, but if she wanted to kill me she'd do it from the kitchen."

"Philly obviously knew too."

"Of course Philly knew, since he was…hey, what are you implying? That Philly's the one sending me the notes?"

"It is a possibility."

"No it isn't. Not Philly."

"All right. That brings us back to the conclusion that you were followed."

"So what do I do?"

"My recommendation would be to get a dash cam, but instead of putting it on the dashboard, install it in the rear window. If someone's following you, they'll show up on the video, including a license number."

Frankly, I had no idea if that would work. I simply felt that I had to tell him *something* to indicate I was taking his case seriously.

"Smart," Mazetta responded. "Where do you get one of those?"

"Any big box store. I can pick one up for you if you like."

"Do it. In fact, get two. One for the limo and one for my Mustang."

Mazetta reached for his wallet, opened it and pulled out a thousand dollar bill, which he handed to me.

I wondered how long it would be after receiving my inheritance from the Palmer Hanley estate before I stopped doing involuntary Three Stooge reactions to the sight of money.

"Will that cover it?" Mazetta asked.

"More than," I said, taking it. "I'll give you a full accounting."

"Just give me the damn cameras."

"Can I take this letter, too? There might be some kind of clue on it."

"Sure, take it. You need any pet food?"

"Right now, no. But I'm thinking about buying a house which will make having a pet easier, so maybe in the future."

"You just make sure *I* have a future. *Capisce?*"

"Yes sir."

Vince Mazetta picked up a cell phone, punched in a number, waited a moment, and then said, "Okay, we're done."

Seconds later Marnie entered the office and smiled while she held the door open for me.

Outside we passed the guard again, who said, "Have a nice day."

I didn't believe him.

As I was escorted out to the parking lot Marnie, handed me a card and said, "Call me if you need to for any reason. I've written my private number on there, too."

"Why would I need to call you?"

"If you have a question you don't want to bother Mr. Mazetta with."

"Okay, thanks, Marnie." Ordinarily I would not be so informal, but I didn't know her last name. If that bothered her, she didn't let on. She smiled again, turned around and disappeared back into the building.

I was nearly to my car, wondering what, if anything, the pasted-up letter in my hand would reveal, when I saw Mazetta's limo pulling into the parking lot.

I decided to wait.

Once it had settled into a spot—the one closest to the entrance—Philly got out from behind the wheel, allowing that side of the limo to rise up a couple inches. Going to the trunk, he opened it and pulled out a bottle of window cleaner and a rag, then started to work on the windshields.

"Hi, Philly," I called, moving toward him.

Instinctively he whipped around, pointing the nozzle of the window cleaner bottle at me like a gun.

"It's Dave Beauchamp. Remember me?"

"Oh, yeah, Beauchamp. The guy with the cluck-bucket."

Our first encounter had included a takeout order from Mr. Clucky's Fried Chicken.

"Sorry," he said, lowering the Windex. "You here to see the boss?"

"I already talked to him, but now I'd like to ask you a question or two."

"About what?"

"About this."

I handed him the letter.

"So you know, huh," he said.

"That's why I'm here. Can you tell me anything about this?"

"Only that I was the one who found it."

"Was it in an envelope?"

"Naw. Just folded and stuck under the wiper blade."

"Where were you while this happened?"

"Whadd'ya mean?"

"I mean it's obvious you weren't in the limo, or even near it, or else you would have seen who left the letter."

"Right. Well, I knew Mr. M was gonna be a while in the Gore store so I went over to this little café that's down the street. If the boss needs me, he calls."

"How long were you at the café?"

"I dunno. Fifteen minutes? Twenty? I had a catchapino."

"A what?"

"Catchapino. You know, coffee with foam on it."

I'm sure he meant *cappuccino*, but Philly wasn't someone I'd relish correcting.

"When I got back to the car, Mr. M was already coming out of the store," he went on. "The letter was there and I didn't get a chance to hide it."

"What do you mean, hide it?"

"After the first one, I've been able to keep most of the others from him."

"How many others are we talking about?"

"Five or six."

"He's gotten five or six threatening letters that you never told him about?"

"I don't like to worry him."

"They were all left on his car?"

"No, the others came in the mail. You ever meet Marnie?"

I nodded.

"Well, she handles Mr. M's mail and pulls those out before he sees them, and then gives them to me."

"Do you still have them?"

"Yeah."

"Can I take them?"

"Why?"

"I'm working on the case."

"I dunno…"

"Look, Philly, why haven't you shown these to Mr. Mazetta?"

"I don't want him to get upset."

"Do you care if I'm upset?"

"No."

"Then there's no reason I shouldn't see them."

He furrowed his brow and then said, "Okay, that makes sense."

Going back to the trunk, he pulled out a black briefcase before slamming the trunk shut again. He opened the case. I was expecting to see a handgun, but in that I was surprised. There were only papers, a few maps, and a banana. Going through the papers, he pulled out six that looked near-ly identical to the one Mazetta had given me and handed them over.

"Did you save the envelopes?" I asked.

"Naw. Why?"

"They might have contained clues as to who is sending these."

"Oh, you mean like DNA on the flap, where they licked it? I saw that on TV."

"That, possibly, but it also might contain fingerprints. So if you get another letter, save the envelope, okay?"

"Sure. I'll let Marnie know, too"

"You're a good man, Philly."

"Really?"

"Really. And thanks."

"Yeah, sure Mr. Beauchamp."

Now it was *Mr.* Beauchamp.

"Take care, Mr. Beauchamp," he said, giving me a wide, crooked grin.

Lassie started barking inside my head, which was appropriate given that I had a strong suspicion I'd just inadvertently adopted a very large puppy.

When I got back to my parent's house, I could hear the laughter coming from inside halfway up the walk.

Some might take this as a good sign. I, on the other hand, had a terrible premonition of what was happening.

My fears were confirmed when I entered and found the lights turned out.

The laughter was coming from the living room.

Stepping closer, I heard the unmistakable *whrrrrr* of an old Super 8 movie projector.

Looking in, I saw a portable screen set up in front of the television, and a six-year-old version of me dressed up as Groucho Marx for Halloween.

That's the most ridiculous thing I think I ever saw, Groucho's voice said inside my head, and I had to agree.

"Um…I'm back," I said through the chuckles.

Hannah turned around.

"Hi, Dave. We've been watching home movies."

"Dad, you didn't show her *that* one did you?"

Dad, who was looking a lot better than when I had left, turned and said, "She got a big kick out of it."

"It was cute," Hannah agreed.

Since I was an adolescent, Dad had been threatening to show the first girl I brought home a movie he shot when I was about two, showing me paddling up the stairs on all fours, stark naked, with Dave junior and the twins taking the starring roles. I had spent most of my prom night in a sweat after my date showed up, but Dad had taken mercy on me then.

There was no mercy now.

"I can run it back if you want to see it, Davy," he said.

"No. I'm fine. Thanks."

Since I still have a problem with blushing, I was glad the room was dark.

Once the white leader with writing on it had run through the gate, Dad shut off the projector and Mom switched on the lights.

"We'll have to do this again sometime," Dad said as he threaded the film for rewinding.

"I'd love to," Hannah replied.

"We should probably get back," I said to Hannah.

"You sure you can't stay for dinner?" Dad asked, prompting a glare from Mom.

"How about we swing by tomorrow for dinner, and by then I'll have the legal files you wanted."

"You've still got the list, right?"

"In my pocket."

"Thanks for doing this."

"Not a problem."

He smiled ruefully. "Oh, I'm pretty sure it is, but I still appreciate it."

It was nearly four o'clock by the time we'd made our goodbyes and left, with the promise of returning tomorrow evening at six. I had plenty of time to swing by a Best Buy to check on those dash cams, but I thought it might be smarter to do a little research online to find out which store had the best price.

"Your father's really nice," Hannah said as we fought our way through the west side traffic.

"You wouldn't want to face him in court, but off the job he's always been a great guy. That's why I was a little alarmed by his comments today. Did you have a chance to look at his prescriptions?"

"Only for a second. I couldn't see anything that would create a problem. But when he came back downstairs after you left, he complained about feeling tingly and a little light-headed. I suggested he cut his blood pressure medicine down to half. If you take too much, it has that effect. And there's no need to be embarrassed about that movie. You were only two at the time. Nobody really thinks *that* way about a little kid."

I couldn't help but shake my head. As much as Hannah had been through in her life—living rough, drugs, being held captive by a cult—she somehow maintained the innocence of a Dickens heroine.

The least horrible way of getting from Cheviot Hills to the Valley was the 405 freeway, which was predictably jammed at this time of day. It was another hour before we arrived at the apartment. Hannah went straight to the kitchen while I studied the letters Vince and Philly had given me. All of them were a smorgasbord of fonts, pitches, and colors, and many displayed a grisly creativity that one rarely finds in death threats.

Live as though today is your last day on earth, because it might be one read.

Another one: *Violets are blue, roses are red; make out a will cause soon you'll be dead.*

One in particular caught my attention because it really *was* made of cut-and-pasted clippings. Under an ad from a grocery store flier for Perfect Friends dog food was a printed line reading, *Soon in Vincent meat flavor.* That made me wonder if the perpetrator was an animal activist who found out Vince was still using horsemeat in his pet food, even though it had been outlawed in California. But having learned firsthand what the Burger Heaven fast food chain had been putting in their patties a few cases ago, I knew there were ways around the law, if you knew whose campaign to contribute to.

After sticking the letters in a file, I went into the kitchen to see if Hannah needed any help with dinner, which she did not. That was good because she is an infinitely better cook than I am.

It was a little after ten when we were both contemplating bed—and even maybe sleeping—that my cell phone rang.

"Dave Beauchamp," I said into it.

"Mr. Beauchamp, this is Philly. You know, Mr. Mazetta's—"

"Yes, I know who you are Philly. What can I do for you?"

"You can find the boss."

"I'm sorry?"

"You can find Mr. Mazetta."

"I'm not following you. I saw Vince earlier today, right before I talked to you."

"Yeah, I know. Then he went poof."

"He did what?"

"Vanished. Disappeared. He's gone, Mr. Beauchamp."

FOUR

Vince Mazetta lived at the end of a narrow road just off Benedict Canyon Drive as it neared Sunset Boulevard. Given the scarcity of street lights in the area, as well as the tall hedge around the property, I could not see much of the house behind the gate. But anything in this neighborhood was bound to be a mansion. Philly was standing right on the other side of the gate, looking only slightly less formidable than the barred barrier. Upon seeing me he opened the gate.

"Thanks for coming," he said through the car window. "Just pull up in front."

Casa Mazetta was even more impressive than I had imagined. It was a brick, Tudor-style manor that would not have been out of place somewhere on the moors of England. After getting out of my Corolla, I looked around on the ground for the footprints of a gigantic hound.

Philly escorted me inside the house, which looked like a private museum with sculptures and paintings displayed virtually everywhere, and expensive-looking rugs covering the hardwood floor. I was taken into the living room which contained a stone fireplace so large I could have stood upright inside it and modern furniture that contrasted somewhat with the wood paneling and ornate trim. One entire wall was a bookcase, filled with leather-bound collectors' editions.

Clearly the pet food business was a profitable one.

A quick examination of the books revealed many of them to be mysteries ranging from Agatha Christie to Walter Mosley.

"Those are mine," a voice said behind me, and I turned around to see a woman standing there.

I suppose I should not have been surprised to see that it was Marnie, but it did throw me a little. She had traded in the man's suit from earlier in the day for a simple pair of slacks and white blouse, which looked spectacular on her.

"Thank you for coming so promptly, Mr. Beauchamp," she said, extending her hand. "You're probably wondering why I'm here this time of night."

"It's not really any of my business," I said.

"It will be. You see, I'm not simply Vince's assistant...I'm also his wife."

Well, that puts a whole new light on things, the voice of Dick Powell commented.

"You're the wife?" I asked, dumbly.

She smiled. "Yes, I'm *the* wife. What has Vince said about me?"

"Nothing specifically. At least nothing in a marital capacity."

"Did he mention I'm not a brilliant cook?"

"Well, he may have said something about that."

"He's right, I'm not. We employ a chef."

Since I remembered Vince once saying he had a grown kid who worked in the film industry, I had to assume Marnie was a second wife. She seemed far too young to be the mother of a Millennial.

"Sit down, please," she said, and I did.

"I should begin by asking when the last time you saw Vince was."

I had all but forgotten Philly was still in the room until he answered, "I was with him up until a few hours ago, then…*pfffffft.*"

"If it's only been a few hours, it might be a little too early to assume that something has happened to him."

"Mr. Beauchamp," Marnie said, "Vince is a creature of habit. He gets up at the exact same time every morning. He leaves for work at the exact same time every morning."

"And if there's a traffic problem on the way that makes him later than usual, he's none too happy, believe me." Philly added.

"He eats lunch in the same restaurant every day and leaves work in the evening at the same time. His schedule never varies. We eat dinner at exactly seven-thirty, after which Vince watches television until turning in at eleven. Even on the weekends he keeps to a basic schedule. If he happens to make an appointment with his tailor, or has a rare dinner out with an associate, he makes certain everybody knows about it and knows where he is. If he is out with someone, he always calls to give me his schedule."

"He mentioned to me that he had a beach house he escaped to when he needed to be alone," I interjected.

"Yes, he has a beach house. I think he's been there three times during our marriage, and while there, he phones every hour or so to make sure everything here is all right. That's his idea of getting away."

"I see."

"I hope you also now see why the fact that we can't find him is so upsetting."

"Please give me all the details."

"Well, he and Philly left work this afternoon at the usual time—"

"Wait a minute. You don't ride with him to and from work?"

"No. Vince wants it that way. He thinks it would look less than professional if the staff saw us coming and going together. Nobody at the plant knows we're married, except for the woman in HR. I have my own car and come and go separately. It works out because some days I either need to run errands or stay a little late."

"All right," I said. "Did anything unusual happen today? Other than Vince's *pfffffft* I mean."

"Frankly, Mr. Beauchamp —"

"Please call me Dave."

"Very well, Dave. The only out-of-the-ordinary occurrence during work hours was your showing up at the plant."

"What about after work hours?"

"I started to drive him home, like usual," Philly said, "but suddenly he said, 'Oh, I forgot something!' I asked him what it was and he told me that his daughter Vickie's birthday was coming up and he had to get her a card."

"Does Vickie live here?"

"No, she's up at Stanford, studying medicine," Marnie said. "Vince really misses having her around, too. She's his youngest and he spoils her a little. He said the thing all college freshmen want most is money so he was going to get her a big card and stuff it with cash."

"I see. Go on."

Philly resumed: "Mr. M told me to pull over at a store that sold cards, so when we passed a drug store, I pulled in. He said he was just going to run in, get a card, and then come right back out, so I should stay put in the car. But he didn't come out. After about twenty minutes I got out of the limo to see if he was in the parking lot anywhere, but didn't see him. I finally went in myself, and asked the clerk if she'd seen anybody that matched his description, but she was busy and just shook her head. I went back out to see if maybe we'd passed each other, and hoped he wasn't standing by the limo all pissed off, but he wasn't. I went back in and searched through the store, but there was no sign of him. I asked a couple more employees, but they didn't know anything. So I tried calling him and just got a message box."

"Is that unusual?" I asked.

"Vince always answers his cell if he recognizes the number," Marnie said. "He would never let a call go unanswered if it was from Philly, or me, or one of his kids, even if he's in the bathroom."

"What did you do when you couldn't get him on the phone, Philly?"

"I hung around another half-hour, running back-and-forth between the store and the car until a security guard came up and wondered what I was doing. I told him I'd lost somebody and described the boss, and he took me to the manager, who I nearly punched out."

"What did the manager do?"

"He made an announcement over the loud speaker asking if anyone's seen a lost little boy!"

"Philly's very protective," Marnie said, struggling to stifle a smile.

"Obviously, the man was mistaken," I told him.

"Damn right he was! I told him who the boss was, and…ohhhh, now I get it." Philly the behemoth actually started to turn red. "The guy asked me to describe Mr. M and I said he was about *this* high." He held his hand up to his belt. "He's, you know, not that tall."

Standing next to Philly, who by my estimation was six-three minimum, Vince would have looked like a toddler.

"Don't worry about it, Philly. It's not your fault. The important thing is whether anybody responded to the announcement."

"Naw. No one."

"And there's nowhere you think he might have gone?"

Philly shook his head. "If you ask me, he was abucketed."

"He was what?"

"I think he means abducted," Marnie said. "But even if that were true the kidnapper would have had to know Vince was going to be there, and how could he? Vince made a spur-of-the-moment decision to stop and get a card. There's no way someone could have been expecting him."

"Unless it was pre-planned that he'd meet somebody at the store," I offered.

"Why would he do that?"

"Obviously, I don't know. But assuming Vince didn't simply skip out on his own, the only other logical option is that someone was tailing the limo, saw it pull into the store's parking lot, and followed Vince inside."

"I would have seen a tail," the big man asserted.

"But it was a busy store, Philly. People come and go all the time. You might very well have seen the tail, if in fact there was one, but you would have assumed it was simply another shopper."

"Shit," he muttered, then, "Oh, sorry, Marnie."

"You're forgiven," she said. "Do you have any advice, Dave?"

"It's likely that the store has security cameras," I said. "If someone approached Vince in the store it might have been captured on tape."

"Let's go look at it then," Philly said.

"The thing is I'm not sure we can demand to see that footage on our own, as private citizens. It would probably take the police."

"I don't want the police involved," Marnie said.

"It's unlikely they'd respond so soon after Vince's disappearance anyway," I told her. "If it was a child or an elder, or someone suffering from a physical or mental condition, the cops would jump right on it. But Vince is a fully cognizant adult, which means he'd have to be missing for a longer period for the police to launch an investigation. On the other hand, if you were to show them those letters Vince received, that might spur them into action."

That did not seem to please her.

"Pardon me for asking, Mrs. Mazetta, but is there a specific reason you don't want to involve the police?"

"If I tell you, will you keep it confidential?"

"Of course I will."

"And please call me Marnie, just like you do at the office. To me 'Mrs. Mazetta' is Vince's first wife, Goldie. She died in a car accident when they were still married and their son, Michael, was about seven years old. I never met her, of course, but Vince still talks about her. Sometimes it's a little like *Rebecca*, where the memory of the first wife colors everything that goes on in the house."

"I'm sorry to hear that, but you still haven't told me why you're hesitant to go to the police."

She looked down at the floor. When she raised her head again a steely gaze had taken over her eyes. "Every television crime show I've ever seen, and every mystery I've ever read, points out that the spouse is always suspect number one in any domestic crime. Is that wrong?"

"The spouse is automatically considered, yes, but—"

"So if I report this to the cops, wouldn't they assume it's all a set-up, and that Philly and I conspired together to get rid of Vince and made up the letters as part of the scheme?"

"Even if that's the point at which they start, I'm certain after investigating further they'll go off into other directions."

"But only after an investigation. I don't want that."

While I could not guess the reason for her reluctance, I sensed there was little use in continuing to argue. "Look, I have a contact who's a detective," I told her. "He trusts me."

Which goes to show what kind of an idiot he is, Robert Mitchum chimed in.

For some reason, "Mitchum" hated me. I have no idea why.

Ignoring him, I said, "How about I run this past my contact?"

"Will he be in charge of the case?"

"No, he's in robbery-homicide. He wouldn't do a missing persons case, but he could give me advice on how to proceed."

She sat for a moment then said, "It doesn't thrill me, but if you think it will help, go ahead. Can you keep Vince's name out of it?"

"I think so. I'll contact him first thing tomorrow but speak hypothetically. Going back to Vince's daughter...what was her name again?"

"Vickie."

"Right. Is it possible that Vince could have gone up to see her instead of sending a card?"

"How would he get there from a drug store?" Philly asked.

He had a point.

"I'm thinking out loud, is all," I said. "I'm trying to make some sense of this. I take it Vickie is Vince's daughter with Goldie?"

"Oh, no, Vickie's mother is named Annemarie. I'm Vince's third wife. He has another son, too, Paul, who's four years older than Vickie, also by Annemarie."

"I should probably talk to Annemarie, then."

"If you can find her. And even if you do, she probably won't be much help."

"Why not?"

"Annemarie, I'm afraid, has more issues than *Life* magazine. When her kids were little she developed a pretty serious addiction to pills. I'm told she nearly burnt down the house one night attempting to fix dinner while blasted on something. That's another reason Vince insists on having a chef. Anyway, Vince divorced her and got custody of Paul and Vickie, and she's been in-and-out of rehab several times. But it never seems to stick. Vince coerced her to try it again earlier this year, with him paying the bill, of course, but sometime last month she left the clinic."

"She was released?"

"No, she simply disappeared one night. Vanished."

"Vanished…like Vince," I said, more to myself than Marnie.

But she heard it.

"If you're trying to sell me on the idea that Vince took off so he could get back together with Annemarie, you can forget it."

"I'm not selling anything, I'm still thinking out loud," I said. "How much contact do you have with Vince's kids?"

"What you're really asking is how I get along with them," she said.

Marnie was very perceptive.

"As well as can be expected, I guess," she went on. "I'm the wicked stepmother, and only two years older than Michael, which means he hardly thinks of me as 'Mom.'"

"What does Michael do?"

"He has a limo service in Orange County."

"That's how Mr. M acquired his wheels," Philly added.

"As for Paul and Vickie, well, like I said, they had a pretty rough time growing up in the Valley of the Dolls, so they learned to rely on each other. They're something of a unified front in regards to me. Both are cordial, but I'll probably always be a bit of an interloper in their eyes."

"One time Vince mentioned having a son in the movie business," I said. "I take it that's Paul."

"Yes. He graduated last year from the USC cinema department. He's an assistant director and doing quite well. He even got me a background role on a George Clooney film, though I think his motivation was simply so he could spend the entire day telling his stepmother where to stand and what to do."

"That must have been awkward."

"Oh, I played along, which I think might have actually impressed him. The thing with all three kids, Dave, is that they're happy as long as their father is happy. Since Vince and I are very happily married, I think they're fine."

"How old is Michael?" I asked.

"Thirty-three," she replied. Then her face broke into a dark smile. "But you're really asking me how old I am, aren't you? Since I'm two years older than Mike, it follows that I'm thirty-five. And Vince is fifty-eight. Philly, I'm not sure about."

"Not sure about what?" Philly asked.

"Your age."

"Oh. As far as I know, fifty-four. Why?"

"Mr. Beauchamp seems to want to know."

I could feel myself starting to blush on the inside, which I hope did not seep outwardly. "It's not that I'm being nosy, Marnie," I said. "I was simply curious how somebody who looks as young as you do knew about *Life* magazine, which you mentioned earlier, but which hasn't been around in either of our lifetimes."

"Hoisted by my own metaphor," she laughed. "Very well, shamus, I have quite a collection of old issues. They're where I get the inspiration for my outfits."

That made perfect sense. I'm glad something did.

The phone rang then. Both Marnie and Philly tensed.

"That might be the kidnapper," Philly said.

"We don't yet know that he's been kidnapped," I offered. "Answer it, Marnie."

She briskly stepped to the phone and picked it up.

"Hello…Oh, god, go to hell!" She slammed the phone down and walked back, her hand over her brow. "I hate telemarketers, especially at this time of night."

"You didn't happen to recognize the voice, did you?" I asked.

"Of a telemarketer? Of course not. Why would I?"

My thought was that it might not have been a real telemarketer, but rather someone running a pretense to see if she was home to accept a subsequent ransom call. Until another call came, though, I decided to keep that thought to myself.

Then I had another thought, not a very pleasant one.

What if Philly was lying about the birthday card, the drug store, the entire thing and was in on Vince's disappearance?

What if Philly knew exactly where Vince was?

Like stuffed inside a limo trunk? a voice said inside my head, and it took me a second to realize it was Bob Hoskins using his *Roger Rabbit* American accent.

Knowing what I knew about Philly and his loyalty, that didn't scan. But neither did the idea that someone disappeared off the face of the earth from a CVS.

Besides…what, exactly, did I really *know* about Philly?

There was only one way to test the theory.

"Philly, would you mind if I examined the limo?" I asked.

"Why?"

"It just struck me that, instead of someone following you, they might have planted some kind of homing signal in the car. That way they'd know where you are at all times."

"Oh. Okay, c'mon outside."

His willingness to show me the car was a good sign…unless he was planning that I join Vince in the trunk.

Using the keychain flashlight I habitually carry, I inspected the interior of the limo as best I could in the dark, and found nothing unexpected. Then Philly opened the trunk.

In addition to the briefcase and bottle of Windex I'd seen earlier, it also contained a fire extinguisher, a set of jumper cables, a tire iron, a cloth shopping bag, a few quarts of motor oil, and a bottle of transmission fluid—the sort of stuff you'd expect to see in the trunk of a well-maintained vehicle.

As opposed to mine.

I made a show of examining every surface, and even picked up the trunk board to look at the spare tire well.

"Okay, it was just a thought," I said, as the exonerated Man Friday closed the trunk. "But if you happen to spot some little device that shouldn't be there, call me, okay?"

"Sure," Philly said.

Marnie was waiting for us at the front door.

"No sign of a bug," I told her.

"So what do we do now?" she asked.

"Like I said, I'll contact my detective friend and keep it casual, no names. Other than that I think the only thing we can do is wait. And if you hear anything at all, call me."

"Do you require a retainer?"

"Vince gave me some money to buy some portable cameras. I still have it. And I promise I'll return whatever I don't use."

She waved her hand in a gesture of unconcern and said, "I'll walk you to your car."

"See you, Mr. B," Philly called from behind.

It was a cool night and honeysuckle was in the air. If this were a film, Marnie and I would stop in the shadow of a tree for some suggestive repartee before ending up in a passionate clinch that would ultimately get both of us in a lot of trouble.

But this wasn't a film, and even if I was by nature a hound dog, I was not so stupid as to make a pass at the wife of a client who might also be a made man.

Being turned into a batch of cat or dog food was not high on my personal goal list.

"Is there anything else you want to know before you leave?" she asked.

"Well, there's kind of a standard investigative question whenever a man doesn't show up on schedule," I said. "I hope you won't find it uncomfortable or insulting."

"You're about to ask me whether Vince has someone on the down-low, right?"

"Um…yeah, that."

"Can I state conclusively, under oath, that Vince has remained one-hundred-percent faithful throughout four years of marriage? No, I cannot. What wife can? But I've never had cause for suspicion. Besides, Vince can have any woman he wants."

"I beg your pardon?"

"Blondes, brunettes, redheads, long-haired, short-haired, professional women, hippies, dumb bunnies, rocket scientists, butches, bitches, you name it. He can have them all."

"I'm sorry, Marnie, but this just isn't scanning."

She glanced up at me and smiled. "They're all *me*, Dave. As I recall, the first time I met you I was Kim Novak. Today I was Katharine Hepburn. I was planning to be Veronica Lake later this week, with the peekaboo hairdo and all. I give him every possible look and attitude so he doesn't have the chance to become bored. You ought to see my Rita Hayworth."

"*Life* magazine?"

"The November tenth, 1947 issue. Shortly after *Gilda* made her a goddess." She smiled again. "Maybe I should have mentioned that there's one more thing on Vince's nightly routine that never varies."

That moment taught me three things about Marnie Mazetta.

One was that she was also an old film buff.

The second was that she must have an incredible wardrobe at her disposal.

The third was she was nobody's fool.

I wondered which realization would prove to be the most valuable.

FIVE

The next morning I left a message on the machine of LAPD Detective Dane Colfax. I didn't know exactly what, if anything, Colfax could do in regards to Vince's disappearance, particularly since I was planning on keeping Vince's identity to myself. Dane had already met him as witness from a previous case. Vince had not liked the experience of being grilled by a cop and told me so in no uncertain terms, so with luck, Dane wouldn't request any details but would simply provide some general advice about tracking a missing person.

When the phone rang a half-hour later, I assumed it was Colfax calling back.

I was wrong.

"Is this Dave…Beauchamp?" a male voice asked, coming close to pronouncing my name correctly.

"It is."

"My name is Michael Mazetta. I'm Vince's son."

"Oh, right. I was talking to your stepmother yesterday."

"Uh huh. Do you know where my father is?"

"No, I don't."

"But you know he's missing, right?"

"I know he appears to have vanished last night."

"Appears to have? He's either MIA or he isn't."

"Mr. Mazetta, all I can tell you is what I've been told. While on his way home from work yesterday your father stopped off at a CVS pharmacy and he's not been seen or heard from since."

"Uh huh. But you would tell me if you did know where he was, right?"

"If I knew where your father was, yes, I would say so."

"Marnie told me you wanted to call the police. You haven't done that, have you?"

"I've not filed a missing persons report because it is not my place to," I said. "That would have to be done by family, but Marnie seems hesitant to do so. What I've done is contact a detective friend of mine simply to ask details about procedure. You know, how long to wait before you should really worry, how to file a report, that sort of thing. I've not heard back from him yet."

I could barely make out a woman's voice in the background, but could not hear what she was saying.

"Just a minute, I'm on the phone," Mazetta called, having turned away from the receiver. "You've not heard back from Dad or you've not heard back from your detective friend?"

"Well, neither, really. To be frank, Mr. Mazetta, I don't think anything sinister has happened to your father. I believe he merely went somewhere and hasn't yet returned."

"Yeah, well, that's not like him. If that is true, though, and he happens to contact you, will you let me know?"

"I will let Marnie know and I'm certain she will share the information with you."

"I really need to be all-in on this matter, too," Michael Mazetta said. "I'd rather you keep me informed personally if and when you hear anything instead of going through Marnie. You can reach me at my company, Loma Limo. It's in Irvine."

Mazetta rattled off a number, which I jotted down.

"It's important to me that Dad be found," he said.

"I will keep you posted, Mr. Mazetta," I said.

"Okay, thanks."

He hung up.

The rest of the day was to be taken up with legal matters. Hannah's schedule included a meeting with our personal lawyer regarding the estate of Palmer Hanley, for which she is the executrix, while I had my own legal odyssey to attend to: stopping by my father's law firm to pick up his files.

The firm of Allen, Garbedian and Lomax occupied three floors in a Century City high-rise. Even though I could now afford to park in the building's garage, I opted to pull into the free one at the shopping center across the street and hike to the office.

Old habits die hard.

The building's lobby, which looked larger than my parents' entire house, was constructed of glass, steel, and marble. Only two other people were in it. But when the doors of the elevator opened, I was suddenly confronted by a half-dozen young paralegals from the firm of Clone, Zombie and Replicant LLC. They each wore identical red neckties over identical white shirts. I was wearing a yellow shirt with no necktie at all, which instantly marked me as a civilian. Getting off at the twelfth floor, I went through the enormous glass doors to the reception desk, where sat a young man who was talking into a headset. He politely held up a finger while he talked. When he was through, he looked up and said, "Yes sir, can I help you?"

"Hi, I'm Carl Beauchamp's son," I said. "I need to pick up a few things for him."

"I believe Mr. Beauchamp is off-site today."

"I know. He's at home. That's why I'm picking things up for him."

"Can I see some ID, please?"

I showed him my license.

"My father asked that I pick up a few files from his office. That's all I want."

"I don't think I can do that without Mr. Beauchamp's permission. Or Mr. Allen's."

Since Dad might be sleeping, or otherwise indisposed, I didn't want to bother him. "All right, let me speak with Mr. Allen."

"Hold on." The guy punched a button on his phone and said into the headset mic, "Hi, Sarah? Could you please tell Mr. Allen that Mr. Beauchamp's son is here and wishes to see him? He wants to be let into Mr. Beauchamp's office. Okay, thanks." He looked up at me and said, "Someone will be out to deal with you shortly. Take a seat, please."

The *please* seemed to stick in his throat.

A couple minutes later, a middle-aged man with perfectly-styled gray hair (including a little curl in front), a perfectly-fitted shirt and silk tie, and shoes so polished they reflected the reception desk, appeared from the back. When he saw me he grinned and held out his hand. "So you're David," he said, pumping my hand. "I'm Len Allen. I've heard so much about you from Carl."

"Really?"

"And I've read about you, too, in the papers. You're quite the gumshoe, apparently."

"I've gotten lucky."

"I didn't see Carl come in this morning. Is everything all right?"

"You don't know, then?"

"Know what?"

"He's had a heart attack."

"Good lord! Is he in the hospital?"

"He was for a bit, but he's home now. It wasn't a major attack."

"I had no idea."

"I'm surprised he or my mom didn't call in with the news."

"They may have and it simply didn't get to my office," Allen said. "I've been very busy."

"Dad asked if I could pick up the files for some of the cases he's working on and bring them home so he can keep working from there."

"Of course, of course. Follow me."

Allen led me through a maze of cubicles and people to a large corner office with my father's name on the wall beside the door. Upon entering, I was not surprised to find it very neat. Even the stack of legal-sized manila folders, piled on one side of the huge wooden desk, was perfectly straight. Pulling out the list Dad had given me, I started to go through them.

The file for Cleerman, the one charged with sexual harassment, was on top, and I found the other four underneath. Three files remained on his desk.

"Mind if I see which ones he asked for?" Len Allen asked, and I handed them to him. As he examined the names on the tabs he nodded silently. Then he said, "He didn't request the Mazetta file?"

Inside my head I heard the sound of screeching car brakes.

"I'm sorry," I said, "the which file?"

"Mazetta. Your father knows the details of the case much more thoroughly than I do, but it has the potential to be a big one."

"Oh, right, I remember him talking about it now," I lied. "Vince Mazetta, the pet food king, right?"

"No, I don't believe so," Allen said, looking through the remaining files on the desk. "Here it is. Our client is named Annemarie Mazetta."

Vince's second wife, whose whereabouts were presumed unknown.

"What's the case?" I asked.

"She's suing a rehab facility at which she resided for a while for alleged physical abuse committed against her."

"What kind of physical abuse?"

"I believe she claims she was raped."

"So he's representing the defendant in one sexual case and the plaintiff in another?"

"It is essential that both sides have good representation, and your father offers some of the best in Los Angeles."

Maybe Dad is right; maybe everything evens out if you look at the big picture of the law.

And maybe that's why I'm still not cut out to be a lawyer.

"I wonder why Dad didn't want me to bring the Mazetta file, too." I said.

"I can't imagine, since rehab clinics have boatloads of money. Perhaps it escaped his mind at the time." Then lowering his voice, he added, "His mind is still functioning, isn't it?"

"Yes, his heart took a hit but his mind is fine."

"Good. Let me see if he made any notes that might explain it." Allen flipped through the contents in the folder, and then said, "Aha, now I understand why he didn't ask for this file. Damn. I thought we had a good case here, too."

"What did you find?"

"The identity of the man Ms. Mazetta accused of raping her while in drug rehab."

"Who was it?"

"Elvis Presley."

"Elvis Presley? *King Creole, Blue Hawaii,* that Elvis Presley?"

"Well, obviously not, since the accusation says the incident in question occurred five months ago. I can't recall exactly when Elvis died, but I'm pretty sure it was longer ago than that." Allen looked at me and smiled. "But you are your father's son. Carl is forever spouting little bits of film trivia around the office. Somehow he keeps all this stuff in his head."

"We're both film buffs. I got it from him."

Allen tossed the Mazetta file down onto the desk. "At any rate, it seems obvious now that Carl didn't mention it because the case is DOA. The worst judge in L.A. County...and I've appeared before him repeatedly... would throw this out in a heartbeat. Anyway, if you've got what you need, I really should be getting back to work."

"Yes, and thank you very much."

"And tell your father for me to stop loafing and get his ass back into the office." He smiled when he said it then added, "Seriously, give him my best and tell him I expect a full recovery."

"I will, thank you, Mr. Allen."

As soon as he had turned and was heading toward the door, I scooped up the Mazetta file again and put it on my stack.

It took me a while to find my way back to the lobby. When I finally found it, I saw that the young man behind the reception desk had been replaced by a young woman. Maybe the guy was taking an early lunch.

Speaking of lunch, it was a little after noon when I got back to the apartment. Hannah was still out, but I didn't fix anything to eat, opting instead to wait for her. I did, however, look through the fridge to see what our choices were.

I have a pet theory that you can discover an awful lot about a person based on what they have in their refrigerator. Traditionally mine has contained little except milk, butter, eggs, sodas, and on occasion some boxed-dinner leftovers. Now, thanks to Hannah, it is fully stuffed with all manner of food in each food group, and a variety of sauces and condiments.

What this tells me about myself is that I'm probably going to be putting on a little weight.

While waiting, I began to peruse the Mazetta file for anything else of value pertaining to my case.

The address line on the information form listed a P.O. Box in the 90049 zip code, which was somewhere on the west side, but Dad had written in beside it, *96 S. Barrington, Apt. 301.*

For occupation, she (or at least someone other than Dad) had written, *Part-time cordwainer.*

If memory served a *cordwainer* was an ancient term for a shoemaker.

Her place of work was listed as "Vegan Leather Emporium" in Brentwood.

Vegan Leather?

Fruitcake, anyone? said the cheery voice of Myrna Loy.

According to the typed-up notes, Annemarie claimed to have had her encounter with Elvis at a clinic in Malibu, which, I suppose, is as good a place as any. The more I read, the harder it was not to laugh, and I had to confess that I would have liked to have seen my dad's face while he was interviewing her.

The clinic was called Start Over, and Dad had jotted down a phone number beside the name.

Only a dummy would pick up the phone, call a rehab facility, and ask to speak with Elvis Presley.

So naturally I picked up the phone.

It was answered on the second ring.

"Start Over Clinic, how may I direct your call?" a woman said.

"Um, well, I'd like to speak with Elvis," I said.

"Elvis?"

"You know, Elvis Presley."

After a pause, she said, "One moment please," and put me on hold.

I should have hung up right then and there, but I felt I at least needed to hold on so I could try to explain and, if necessary, apologize.

I had my explanation ready to go in my head when I heard the call taken off hold.

"Howdy," a man's voice said.

"Oh, uh, hi, who's this?" I asked.

"This is the King."

It was his voice, and for once it wasn't inside my head.

"This is…Elvis Presley?"

"It ain't Elvis Costello, man. Now, you called me so you better tell me what I can do for you."

Assuring me I had not gone completely insane would have been a nice start.

SIX

"Hey, c'mon, man, say somethin'" Elvis went on. "Hound dog gotchur tongue?"

"Uh…"

"At least tell me who I'm talkin' to."

"My name is Dave Beauchamp."

"Mr. Beauchamp, pleased to know you."

"Uh…likewise."

"So, do I pass?"

"I'm sorry?"

"Do I pass?" the man asked, his voice suddenly changing.

"Pass for what?"

"For the King. For whatever event you want to hire me for. Look, Mr. Beauchamp, you are calling me about an Elvis gig, right?"

"Oh jeez, you're an impersonator!"

There was a long pause, after which he drawled, "Yes, what did you think? Why did you call if you didn't want to hire the best Elvis impersonator in L.A.? In fact, who gave you this number?"

"Maybe we should start over, Mr.…."

"Sandburg. Evan Sandburg."

"Mr. Sandburg, my father is an attorney who is, or at least was representing a client named Annemarie Mazetta, and—"

"Oh, god, no, man, no! Not her! Anyone but her!"

"Um…"

"Look, Mr. Beauchamp, I'll have to call you back. I can't monopolize the office line. Give me your number."

I did and he hung up. I figured there was at best a fifty-fifty chance he'd actually call back, which is why I was surprised when the phone rang only a minute later.

"Mr. Beauchamp?" Sandburg said. "Okay, I can speak freely now. What's Annemarie claiming I did to her now?"

"Well, rape, actually."

"Oh, mercy! I never should have put the costume on for her."

"Do you think we might back up just a little bit?" I asked. "Please tell me what you do at the clinic."

"I'm an orderly here," he said. "It's the day job and I do Elvis gigs whenever I can get them. Usually people call me directly which is why I was surprised to get the call here at work. I assumed it was a former patient. We get some big names through here, and I try to do my act for them. See, it has an anti-drug message. I say, 'Don't do drugs, man, just look what happened to me.'"

The last part was spoken as Elvis.

"How do the patients take that?"

"Usually they laugh. Sometimes it's the only laugh they get while they're incarcerated here. Though one or two had to be assured they weren't seeing a ghost, or having the DTs or something. That's how good I am."

"What was your experience with Annemarie Mazetta?"

"Oh, lordy. She dang near threw herself at me, like she wanted to have my baby. I tried telling my supervisor, but he dismissed it because, well, you know what they say about the customer always being right. Only the doctors here are allowed to treat the patients like they're not the boss. When she found out I really wasn't interested in a relationship with her, she blew a gasket and tried to attack me physically. I'm King-sized, Mr. Beauchamp, six feet tall and 170 pounds, and it was all I could do to keep her from knocking me silly. She started throwing threats at everybody after that, and they finally had to kick her out. My next performance review wasn't any picnic, either, I can tell you that."

"Did my father, Carl Beauchamp, ever contact you regarding Annemarie?"

"No, you're the only person outside of the clinic I've talked to about this. Now she's claiming I *raped* her? Aw, man! The only time I ever touched her was when I pushed her away as she tried to scratch my eyes out. Do I need to get my own lawyer?"

"I don't think so. My dad's law firm is not taking her accusation seriously."

Though if they knew the best Elvis impersonator in L.A. was the defendant, they might.

"That's a relief." He turned back into Elvis long enough to say, "Bad publicity, man. So, should I assume this means you don't have a job for me?"

"I don't, sorry," I said. "But if anything changes, I'll be sure get back in touch."

"Thank yuh," Elvis said. "Thank yuh vurrra much."

He hung up.

Sometimes I wonder what it's like to live in a normal universe.

It was nearly two-thirty when Hannah returned, and I was hungry.

"Hi, honey," she said, coming in and dropping her purse on the couch. "This executrix stuff is a little more complicated than I thought it would be."

"Have you eaten?" I asked.

"There were donuts at Mr. Neale's office, so I'm not starving," she said. Richard Neale was our personal attorney. "Haven't you had lunch?"

"Not yet."

"Dave, you have to eat."

"I know, and I want to. I'll open a can of soup. Since Mom is probably fixing a big dinner tonight, eating light now might be good."

The soup was nearly heated when she came in, peered into the pan, and said, "That does smell good. Is there enough for two?"

Knowing that she was probably going to ask that, I had already opened two cans of pub-style chunky chicken.

We had only just begun to eat when the phone rang. It was Dane Colfax from the LAPD calling back.

"How's the missus?" he asked.

"We aren't legal yet, but we're working on it," I told him. "But she's fine. Thanks for asking."

"So, how do you propose to ruin my day this afternoon?"

I went through the story of Vince Mazetta's disappearance and the threatening letters for him—omitting Vince's identity—and he listened patiently. After giving him just the facts, I concluded with, "I'm not sure how to proceed with this."

"Knowing how you seem to get down with the rich and famous in town, is your mysterious missing man a celebrity?"

"This time no, not really. Let's say established, but not famous."

"Then filing a missing person's report would be the place to start."

"Right."

"But you're not going to, right?"

"The man's wife doesn't want to."

"Why not?"

"She's afraid she'll be suspected."

"Of what?"

Now that was a good question I hadn't considered before. Why would Marnie Mazetta be afraid she'd be suspected of kidnapping Vince? What would be the point of a spouse kidnapping her husband?

There was more to this than Marnie was letting on.

"If you want my honest opinion, it sounds like your guy took a powder," Dane said. "If the wife doesn't want to go through us, tell her to call the bank and report hubby's credit cards stolen so they get turned off. He'll probably surface in a day or so. If he doesn't, then she'd better call the professionals."

"I'll pass that along to her," I replied. "Thanks, Dane."

"Sure. Stay out of trouble. Oh, who am I kidding?"

After getting off the phone with Colfax, I called Marnie at her office.

"I'm not buying his skipping out," she said after I passed along the detective's wisdom. "Don't you have anything else?"

"Nothing concrete."

"Don't say concrete, okay?"

"Um, sorry. But since you brought this up, I have a delicate question, Marnie. Your answer might have a lot of bearing on the case."

"What is it?

I took a breath and said: "Is Vince really in the outfit, or is it an act?"

There was a long silence, after which she replied, "Hold on a second while I close my door."

The phone was laid down and I could hear her secluding herself in the office before her voice came on again.

"Okay, Dave, the first thing you have to understand is that Vince knows everybody. When we first started dating we'd be in a restaurant and movie stars would walk up to our table to say hi to him. One time we were someplace and Madonna walked in, and every head turned her way, but she spotted Vince and made a beeline over to him to give him a big hug. I later learned that a lot of this came from his charity work, where he met a lot of other important people and celebrities. The point I'm trying to make is that in Vince's case it is not just an idle expression. He knows ev-er-ee-body. That includes some of the L.A. family. He used to play poker with a couple of Peter Milano's guys. Vince even allowed Milano to use his name as a threat and tell his minions that, if anyone stepped out of line, their headstones would be little tin cans in the pet food aisle of the supermarket."

"But none of that's true, right?"

She laughed. "The worst thing you'll find in our food is horsemeat, but that's only for export. They no longer allow it here. But according to Philly, those threats were effective. He said there was never more harmony among the rival organizations and families as when people believed they either toed the line or would end up in a can of Real Meat Pâté. All this was a little before my time, though."

"Vince gave me a list of alleged goombahs that he thought might be sending those letters. If he's not a real insider, why would those who are worry about him?"

She sighed heavily. "Okay, look, I never said this, but when you reduce it to the essence, Vince is a little bit of a conman. He doesn't run his scam to defraud anyone, he just pretends to be something he's not. Lots of people do that. But the key to making any kind of con work is convincing others you are something you're not. Vince might have succeeded too well."

After giving her as much comfort as I dared that Vince was probably fine, I hung up.

"Something's just not right," I said, more to myself than to Hannah who was hovering around me.

"I'm sure you'll be able to figure it out," she said. "What time do we have to leave to get to your folks' house by six?"

"Five-fifteen at the latest. Traffic's always bad that time of day."

"Do I have time for a shower?"

"I think so."

"Want to help?"

"We don't have *that* much time."

Twenty minutes later Hannah was scrubbed, dewy, and devastatingly pink, with her red hair bushing out as it dried. She managed to tame it somewhat with a brush, but she still had that semi-wild, windblown look.

"Leave it like that," I told her. "I like it."

I liked to look at it so much, in fact, that I nearly forgot to grab Dad's work folders. I included the one concerning Annemarie Mazetta, hoping he might be able to provide some information about her, but also planning to claim I had taken it by accident if its presence in the stack created an issue.

Traffic was surprisingly light and dinner proved surprisingly pleasant. Dad was looking and sounding better, and Mom was on her best behavior, serving up the roast chicken and homemade mashed potatoes (something I had not enjoyed in quite a while) with a smile. Even when Dad and I would get sidetracked on film trivia, she brought us back around to conversation that "meant something to others" with gentility.

After we had finished eating, we all helped clear the table though only Hannah stayed in the kitchen with Mom for more gossip. Dad and I went into the front room.

"Here are your files," I said, handing them over.

"Put them beside the chair," he said, sinking into his recliner, looking suddenly tired.

"You okay?"

"Yeah, yeah, I'm all right. The thing is, when something happens that forces you to take it easy, your routine gets all screwed up. I usually walk a lot, both here and at work, but I've been stuck on my butt for a few days and it's catching up with me."

"I can arrange to get a treadmill, if you like."

"I hate those things. You never get anywhere."

"Well, that's kind of the point."

"If I decide I need one, I'll let you know."

"Mind if I ask about another of your cases? One you didn't request I get the file for?"

"What case is that?"

"Annemarie Mazetta."

Dad's eye roll would have made Vincent Price envious.

"She was like a guy having carnal relations with cashews," he said.

"She was what?"

"Fucking nuts."

Hey, that's not bad! the voice of Milton Berle declared.

"God only knows how she found us," he went on (Dad, not Milton Berle). "At first it looked like she might have a case. But the more I talked to her the more I realized she was marching to the beat of 'Dance of the Cuckoos.' It was all the drugs, probably. There are plenty of people in rehab who only pretend to quit, but still keep using even while they're in the place. Do you know who she claimed assaulted her?"

I nodded. "Elvis Presley."

"How'd you know?"

"Mr. Allen told me. He sends his best, by the way. He was quite surprised to hear of your illness."

Dad smiled. "That means Keller didn't tell him. I wondered whether or not the little rat would keep it to himself."

"You've lost me."

"I've known Len Allen forever. He's good people. But he hired this assistant, Patrick Keller, who's smart as hell and highly efficient, but who has his own agenda. Controlling the information that comes into the office is one of the items on it. I called in myself yesterday morning and asked to talk to Len, but only got as far as Keller. I told him why I wasn't coming in and asked him to inform everyone, but gee, I guess it just slipped his mind. He's probably waiting for me to die."

"You really think he's that cutthroat, Dad."

He shook his head. "You're a good boy, Davy. You always were a good boy. But you have this terrible flaw. You trust people."

"If it's any consolation, I'm getting over it."

"It was bound to happen. Why are you asking after a crazy woman anyway?"

"Because her former husband is a client of mine."

"Oh, good god," he said, half-laughing. "Los Angeles is one of the planet's biggest cities and smallest worlds."

"Do you remember anything in particular about Annemarie?"

"Outside of the fact she was nuttier than a pecan tree in October? No. When she made the accusation against the clinic, I listened because...well, you never know. There're always stories about private hospitals and the like. But then she started screaming that *Elvis* had raped her, well that was the deal-breaker. I didn't bother listening to anything more. If she'd said a celebrity who's still alive I might have had it checked out, but a guy who's been dead since the Carter administration? After that I figured the carriage drive didn't go all the way up to the front porch of Tara so I stopped taking her calls."

"I'll just take this file back then," I said.

The truth was I did not want to bother him with what I had discovered about the rehab clinic's resident King of Rock 'n Roll. Plus my own careful combing of the file might reveal something valuable to my case.

I offered to go through the other files with Dad, to familiarize myself with them, but he waved the idea away. I could see he was getting tired. Hopefully he'd remembered to take his medicine.

"I'll look at all this stuff tomorrow, and if I need you to help me with anything, I'll let you know," he said. Then he began to study my face. "Okay, something's on your mind, Davy. I can always tell. What is it?"

"Dad, you know I can't tell you what to do."

He nodded. "That's your mother's job."

"But maybe you'd be happier if you did retire now, even though you've got two more years to go before you get full benefits. I mean, would the Social Security money make that much difference?"

"Probably not, but money never hurts, either. I won't lie and tell you I'm not thinking about it, Davy. The problem is I don't know what the hell I'd do with myself."

"You could write articles for nostalgia magazines."

"I've already done that."

"I know, but now you could do it full time. Or maybe you could write a book."

"Who would publish it?"

"Well, start your own publishing house. Call it Simon and Shyster."

"Simon and *what*?" he said, and a second later he began to laugh. He laughed himself into a coughing fit. I reached out to him, concerned that I'd provoked something bad, but he waved me away, still coughing and laughing. "Simon and Shyster indeed," he said when the coughing subsided. "Davy, I take back what I said about your being a good boy. And tomorrow I'm going to call Len and have him trademark that name!"

What I wished I could do was reassure him that he would never have to worry about money for the rest of his life since I was a handful of signatures away from becoming stinking rich. But this was not the time.

"Would you mind getting me a glass of water?" he asked.

"Sure thing."

I went into the kitchen where Mom and Hannah were clucking like two chickens on their night off. When Mom saw me she asked, "How is he?"

"Tired. He wants a glass of water."

Mom quickly pulled down a glass and filled it, then handed it to me.

At that moment my cell rang.

"I'll take it to him," Hannah said, taking the glass from me.

Looking at my phone, I recognized the number.

"Hi, Dane?" I said upon answering.

"Beauchamp, what is it with you?" he asked.

"What do you mean?"

"You just can't get through the day without turning over a body, can you?"

"What are you talking about?"

"I'm talking about a dead body that was found under the Malibu pier, a corpse with a name I recognized from your last case. Mazetta."

Aw, *jeez*! While I was trying to figure out how to offer help to Marnie, Vince had gotten killed. What's more, my efforts to keep from mentioning his name to Colfax proved tragically redundant. "How did he die?" I asked.

"*He* didn't."

"But you just said Vince was dead."

"I said we found a body. I didn't say it was Vince Mazetta."

"Dane, I'm lost."

"It's not your cat food guy unless he's into wearing casual dresses to the beach."

Oh, jeez…was it *Marnie's* body that was found?

"Dane, was the corpse thirty-five, slender, blonde, with movie-star looks?"

Mom tensed suddenly, overhearing the word *corpse*.

"Beauchamp, would you stop playing twenty questions and listen?"

"I'm listening."

"The body we found was fiftyish, dark-haired, and had track scars on her arms. She's been ID'd as Annemarie Mazetta."

When the shock abated, I asked what had happened to her.

"It looks like she was strangled."

A snowball formed in my stomach as I realized, despite Marnie's protestations of her husband's charitable, nonviolent nature, the reason Vince might want to disappear.

SEVEN

One a.m. came and went and I was still sitting up in my living room trying to figure out what was going on, and what I was going to do about it. Hannah tried to get me into bed three times before giving up. The fully-leaded root beer, my third of the evening, was not helping me drowse off.

I ran through this mess of a case for the who-knowseth time.

Act one: Vince gets threatening letters.

Act two: Vince vanishes in plain sight.

Act three: Vince's former wife turns up dead on the beach.

Whether this would be a three-act or five-act play was an open question.

I was more than willing to take suggestions from any of my cranial "helpers," though they all appeared to be enjoying a good night's sleep. When a voice finally came it was not one of the Hollywood Victory Caravan.

Some years back I became acquainted with Jack Daniels, a bestselling thriller writer who lives in Santa Monica. Even though it sounded like a gag, Jack Daniels was his real name, though he published his hugely successful "Tory Poacher" novels under a pseudonym. It's a name you'd recognize, too. Occasionally Jack and I meet for dinner, usually in one of his beloved British pubs, which proliferate the nearer you get to the coastline. More commonly we talk by phone. In the past Jack has asked me for details about how a private investigator conducts his business, while I've called upon him to try and make sense out of a string of unconnected facts using his writer's imagination.

It was a good deal for both of us, and I've grown to like Shepherd's pie, if not the auburn-colored, barely-carbonated, sweetish British ales that give his life meaning.

It was Jack's voice that had popped into my mind.

Dear boy, it began in clipped British tones, *this one seems elementary. The dead woman was the author of those letters. She wanted to cause her ex-husband grief by idly threatening him. The loyal henchman of the ersatz Mafioso found out about it and dispatched her. The only question is whether the current wife is involved.*

I knew this wasn't really a theory from Jack himself, though I suspected he might make a similar deduction if asked. I had formulated the theory and projected Jack's voice onto it.

Why?

Because I didn't want to be the one who contemplated it.

But now that it had risen to the surface, I could not deny that it made sense. Philly certainly looked like the kind of guy who was up to the task of murder, and there's no question he was loyal to Vince. And based on the testimony of everyone who knew Annemarie, she was crazy and vindictive enough to threaten her former husband, just for fun.

The wild card was Marnie's involvement, if any.

Still, there was a hole within that theory: it did nothing to explain what had happened to Vince.

I must be getting tired since the voices were engaging in dreamlike conversations. Maybe I was already asleep and didn't know it.

Maybe with you, nobody can tell the difference.

Shut up, Mitchum.

Getting off the couch, soda can in hand, I stopped when I saw Hannah, stark naked, standing in the hallway.

Go ahead and call me a male pig, but the little bit of weight she had shed since leaving the oppressive confines of the Temple of Theotologics gave her a body to die for.

Fine, you're a male pig, the voice of Katharine Hepburn snapped inside my head. *Anything else I can help you with?*

"This is the last time I'm going to ask you to come to bed, Dave," Hannah said.

"Last time's the charm," I replied, setting the root beer can back down and following her into the bedroom.

* * * * *

Despite the fact that it was later than usual when I awoke, I did not feel refreshed. In fact Hannah, who was already up, had to come back into the bedroom and shake me out of a nightmare.

"You were crying out," she told me, once I'd forced open my eyes.

"Did I say anything?" I asked through a yawn.

"Not words. You were making a high-pitched cry like you were really scared."

"Bad dream."

"Want to tell me about it?"

"Not really. You know how dreams are. They don't make much sense once you're awake."

What I remembered of it was being shoved inside a car trunk that suddenly turned into a bus with very cramped seats. Someone was leaning on me: a woman. I was trying to push her into her own seat but stopped when I realized she was dead. Then we were back in the trunk, both of us, and she was bleeding on me, and that's when I screamed in the dream.

Apparently outside of the dream, too.

"It sounded bad," she said.

"Don't worry, I'll be fine," I told her, sliding out from under the covers. "Do you have anything up for today?"

She smiled at my lap and said, "Not yet."

"Would you mind coming with me?"

"Any time. You know that."

"I mean would you mind accompanying me to a place."

"Where are you going?"

"It's a rehab facility in Malibu called Start Over."

I could see her tensing. "Why are you going there?"

"It's for the case I'm working on. Vince Mazetta's ex-wife was a patient there and she's just turned up dead. I'm hoping to get information about her."

"Why do you want me to go?"

"Because with your medical training and experience, you'll know the terminology used for anti-drug programs. I might need to have some translating done. You can also tell me if you feel there's something not quite right about the place. But look, if you don't want to go, that's okay, too. I understand."

"I'll go," she said finally, "as long as we don't spend all day there."

"We won't. It might even be a wasted trip if no one wants to talk, but at least we'll get to see the ocean."

There were only three ways to get from Studio City, our little love-chunk of the San Fernando Valley, to Malibu. One was by helicopter, which was out of the question. Another was by taking the "low-road": Interstate 10 to the Pacific Coast Highway, then northwest about twenty miles. I opted for the third way—the "high-road"—which entailed taking the 101 freeway to Topanga Canyon Boulevard, then cutting south through a much narrower but far more scenic roadway to PCH. From there it was up the coast for only another few miles. Usually the low-road led to guaranteed traffic jams, while the high-road ran the chance of getting stuck for miles behind a large, slow truck on Topanga, with no escape. That was still worth the risk.

It turned out to be the right choice given the surprising lightness of traffic and the absence of trucks. We got to the coast highway in a record fifty minutes.

I made it out there in a flash, at two in the morning, Humphrey Bogart said inside my brain, *just in time to see the Sternwood limo pulled out of the surf.*

Yeah, well, funny thing, Bogie: it's harder to navigate L.A. when you don't have time-condensing lap-dissolves on your side.

Start Over Clinic was not difficult to find. The difficult part was getting past the guard at the security booth, who had to turn sideways to get his shoulders through the door.

"Yes sir," the guy said. "What can I do for you?"

"Um, well, I was rather hoping you'd let me in," I said.

"And you are…?"

"Beauchamp. Dave Beauchamp."

"Your reason for being here?"

"Well, you see, it's like this…"

Now, for anyone who wishes to become a private investigator, here's a tip: figure out your cover story in advance. Obviously, I had not done that, which meant my only remaining option was to be as naturally quick-witted as, say, Jim Rockford.

But that's television.

I knew my reason for being here, but saying, *You see, officer, I just wanted to snoop around for a bit in hopes of talking to an Elvis imperson-ator about a mysterious death*, did not seem like a winning plan.

"Sir?" the guard prompted.

What do I do? I thought furiously.

Then it hit me, and it was almost the truth.

"I'm working with the attorney representing a former patient here, a woman named Annemarie Mazetta, and—"

"You said Mazetta?" the guard interrupted.

"I did."

"Wait a minute."

He dashed back into the guard booth and got on the phone.

Clearly he'd been tipped off to respond if he heard the name Annemarie Mazetta.

He returned with a half-sheet of paper that had *Visitor* bannered across it.

"Mind showing me your ID, Mr. Beauchamp?" he asked.

"Not at all."

After wrestling out my wallet from underneath me and suddenly under-standing the advantage of wearing a jacket with a breast pocket, I handed him my license, which he scanned and handed back.

"Thank you, sir. You have to understand, we sometimes have high-profile people staying here, and there have been instances of reporters and paparazzi trying to sneak in under assumed credentials."

"I understand."

The guard told us to follow the road up to the largest building, park in any available visitor space, and then check in with woman at the desk who would direct us to the office of the clinic's managing director, Wyatt Worsley.

At least I think it was Wyatt Worsley. When your name sounds like *Wyatt Worsley*, there's always the possibility of error.

I thanked him and drove up.

"Are we going to have to meet with this guy?" Hannah asked.

"I don't see any way around it," I said. "But don't worry. I know enough about Annemarie's accusation to be able to hold a conversation. Then we'll take our leave of Wyatt Worsley and…oh, I don't know…maybe get *lost* on the premises, just wandering around until we find the guy I really want to see."

Start Over Clinic was the epitome of a generic building: wide, squat, and white. It could have been anything from a supermarket to a nuclear laboratory. But perched on a cliff with the ocean on one side, and mountains on the other, it offered a spectacular view. After parking, we went to the large glass doors in front which opened to let us in.

New Age music pervaded the lobby, which was austerely furnished but had a trickling waterfall built into one wall. A professional-looking woman in a smart, dark blue pants suit and mouthwash-ad smile greeted us.

"Are you Mr…." (she glanced down at a slip of paper) "… Bowchamp?"

"Beauchamp," I said.

"Sorry."

"Not a problem. This is my assistant Ms. Skaal."

"Hi," Hannah said, glancing around.

"I'm Bethany Proust, Mr. Worsley's assistant. Let me take you to him."

Wyatt Worsley's office was located at the end of a labyrinth of white walls and closed doors. The man himself was on the short side and not quite fat, but inflated-looking. Facially he resembled Dom DeLuise.

"Mr. Beauchamp," he said, "it's a pleasure to finally meet you."

"Finally?" I asked.

"After the correspondence from your office."

"Oh, right. My father, actually, was the one who handled the paperwork. We, uh, work together. He's tied up in court today so here I am."

Ooohh, you're such a liar! the childish, petulant voice of Joe Besser shouted in my head.

"Sit down, please," he bade us. Hannah and I each took one of the overstuffed guest chairs, while he seated himself behind his large desk. "Now, then, Mr. Beauchamp, why are you here?"

I smiled. It was not an attempt to intimidate the man in an I-know-something-you-don't way, even though I did. It was to give me cover while I considered how much to reveal to him regarding Annemarie Mazetta.

My normal philosophy is to not share any more information than is absolutely necessary with anyone regarding a case, including the police. Since this man was hardly the police, it should not have been a problem. But something was forcing me to deliberate.

"Are you taking the fifth, Mr. Beauchamp?" Worsley asked.

"No, no, sorry," I said. "Actually I am here to let you know that Ms. Mazetta's suit against the clinic is being dropped."

Wyatt Worsley leaned back in his chair and nodded. "Someone has finally talked some sense into her."

"I think I can state conclusively that you will not hear from her again."

"Well, that is good news. Is there anything else?"

"Actually, yes," I said, having finally thought of a reason to explain our presence. "My purpose for coming out here was to speak with a Mr. Evan Sandburg and give him the news directly, since he was the primary defendant named in the suit."

"I see. Well, I'm sure Evan will be happy to talk with you." Worsley picked up his desk phone and said into it, "Bethany, see if the King is on the premises and available, would you?" Then he hung up.

"The King?" Hannah asked.

"It's our little joke. It will become clear once you meet him. I presume, Mr. Beauchamp, that you will be following up this visit with official notification in writing that the case is being dropped."

"Oh, yes, of course, certainly," I said, making a mental note to ask Dad about it.

The phone buzzed and Worsley picked it up. "All right, thank you." Turning to us he said, "Mr. Sandburg is in the employee cafeteria, but I can summon him here if you like."

"How about if I go to him? I don't want to disturb his meal time."

"Isn't it a little early for lunch?" Hannah asked.

"Like a hospital, we have staff on duty around the clock," Worsley said. "Evan comes in very early in the morning and leaves mid-afternoon. That way he has his evenings free for his gigs…which will become clear when you meet him. I'll have Bethany take you to the cafeteria."

Within seconds Bethany Proust reappeared and ushered us out of the office, back through the labyrinth, and eventually into an austere, sterile looking lunchroom. "That's him over there," she said, pointing to a man seated alone at a long table.

Her identification was hardly worth the effort.

I'd recognize Elvis anywhere.

As we approached the man with the long sideburns, a suspiciously black pompadour, and hospital blues, he looked up at us and cocked his head. A half-eaten cheeseburger sat on his plate, next to a few thin, pale, industrially-cooked French fries. He had not misrepresented himself over the phone. Most Elvis impersonators I've seen looked like they're dressed for a Halloween party, and nothing more. Evan Sandburg looked so much like him he might have been a close relative...or an illegitimate son.

"Mr. Sandburg," I said, "might I speak with you for a moment?"

"Who are you?" he asked.

"I'm Dave Beauchamp. We spoke on the phone."

"Oh, right." Then slipping into Elvis he said, "You got a gig for the King after all?"

"Not exactly, but I'd still like to talk to you."

Sandburg gestured for us to take a seat, and then said, "You gonna introduce me to this lovely young lady?"

"This is Hannah Skaal," I said, as she looked down demurely. "She's working with me on the Annemarie Mazetta case."

He shuddered. "You told me I didn't need a lawyer."

"You don't. The good news is the case is being dropped."

"That is good news," he said, then took a King-sized chomp out of his cheeseburger. "Through a full mouth he added, "If you're hungry, I can recommend these."

"Maybe later," I said. "I also have some bad news. Annemarie Mazetta is dead."

Evan Sandburg's Elvis face took on an expression of genuine compassion. "Oh. Then I guess I shouldn't have spoken ill of her yesterday. What happened to her?"

"It appears she was murdered."

Now the look of compassion morphed into one of apprehension.

If the real Elvis had been this expressive he might have had a better movie career.

"I hope you don't think I had anything to do with it," Sandburg said.

"That's not why I'm here. I'd like you to tell me anything you remember about her beyond what we discussed on the phone."

"Well, I suppose saying she was crazy doesn't help you much."

"Any corroborating details would be better."

"She had bad breath."

That little problem has been solved, said the voice of Peter Lorre.

"Anything else?"

"Now, you understand that I'm not a doctor, no degree, or anything like that. But she struck me as the kind of person who traded one addiction for another."

Even without looking at her, I could feel Hannah tensing up beside me. In the past she had confessed to me her fear that she was the same way, having swapped out reliance on drugs for reliance on a mind-and-behavior control cult, and, before I confessed my genuine love for her, reliance on that for reliance on sex with me. Under the table, I took her hand and gently squeezed it.

Sandburg went on: "My understanding is that she had an unhappy marriage and that started her on booze, and then later she turned to drugs, including the really bad stuff, like meth."

"Did she go into specifics about her marriage?"

"Only that her husband acted like Vito Corleone but was a cheapskate who wouldn't give her the things she wanted, and was always on her case about the booze and drugs."

"But since she was here in rehab, she must have wanted to get off of those," I ventured.

"I don't know what she wanted to do exactly," Sandburg said. "But she implied that if she did she'd come into a big payday."

"Someone was going to pay her to kick the habit?"

He popped the last bit of cheeseburger into his mouth and uttered: "Mm-hmm." After swallowing, he went on. "Her husband, the Godfather. It was kind of like a prize, or a reward, or something. Positive reinforcement, you know? But she wasn't having an easy time of it. I tried to help, but…well, I told you how that turned out."

"Do you know exactly what set her off regarding you?"

"Regarding the accusation, you mean? I told you about that. When she began to come after me I tried to dissuade her, but I don't think I did it the right way. Fact is I think I really screwed the pooch. See, I put my entire King outfit on and went to her room and sang to her a little because, well, despite everything she seemed lonely and vulnerable. I was trying to cheer her up, but in hindsight I probably shouldn't have done the scarf bit."

"The scarf bit?"

"You know, at the end of a concert, the King would come down into the audience and take off his scarf and drape it around the neck of a woman while he sang just to her, like she was the only woman in the world. I usually pick the oldest woman because they get the biggest kick out of it. Anyway, I went into Annemarie's room one night and sang 'Are You Lonesome' and did the scarf bit, and…oh, man. *Big* miscalculation. She wrapped herself around me like an octopus. I got away but, anytime I'd see her in the hallway after that, I'd have to turn and run. Then I tried to reason with her, let her down gently, but instead she got hard and angry. That's when she started accusing me of things and finally got physical. What's that line about a woman scorned? Oh, man!"

"What medication was she given while she was here?" I asked.

"Benzos. Just about everybody gets benzos."

"What are benzos?"

"Benzodiazepines," Hannah said. "They're anti-anxiety drugs, and not something to mess with. They can be addictive on their own."

"Was Annemarie still taking those when she left?" I asked.

"She left in kind of a hurry, so chances are she was," Sandburg replied. "Look, folks, I don't want to be rude, but I need to get back to my shift pretty soon."

"All right," I said, rising and shaking his hand. "You've been very helpful, thank you. And if the opportunity arises that I require the presence of the King, I will definitely give you a call."

"I do birthdays, bar mitzvahs, and clambakes." He handed me a business card.

As we were leaving the lunchroom Hannah asked, "What's a clambake?"

"It's a party on the beach, but more importantly, at least to him, it's the name of an Elvis movie. What did you make of the guy?"

"He seemed nice, but I've never understood people who want to be someone else. I mean, isn't being yourself hard enough?"

"I think that's the point, Hannah. For some people being themselves is too hard, so they try another personality on for size."

There seemed to be a lot of that going on lately.

I'd gleaned as much as I was going to, so we took our leave. As we were driving away from the Start Over Clinic, Hannah asked, "So, was this trip worthwhile?"

"Well, I found out that it's one thing to call a person crazy in the abstract, but Annemarie Mazetta really did seem to have some serious mental health problems. It sounds like she was a danger to herself and others."

"How did she die?"

"Dane Colfax said it appeared she was strangled. Not to change the subject, but look out there, look at the ocean. I think I called it earlier when I said this view alone would make the trip worthwhile."

The expanse of blue, dotted with a variety of small boats every here and there, was the very image of tranquility. I suddenly understood why Jack Daniels lived near the water.

"It is beautiful," Hannah said, "and who knows? When we get our money, maybe we can buy a boat."

"I don't know anything about sailing."

"Neither do I. But it's strange. When I was at…that place, they made such a big deal of helping you achieve inner peace through workshops, lecturing, and punishment if necessary. But all you really have to do is look at the ocean."

Hannah fell silent until we were back on the less peaceful Topanga Canyon Boulevard, headed home, and then said, "Is it possible for someone to strangle themself?"

"Um, I think it's possible, yes. Why?"

"Well, you said this woman was a danger to herself and others. Maybe she killed herself."

I had to admit *that* had never even entered my mind.

But then something else did, and I actually cried out.

"What's the matter?" Hannah asked.

"Oh, jeez..."

"Dave, what is it?"

"I can't speak to the feasibility of someone actually taking a rope or a belt and strangling themself," I said. "But I can imagine that it would not be all that difficult for someone to strangle another person with a scarf."

"A scarf?"

"Yeah...like the ones Elvis Presley used to drape around the necks of women in his audiences."

EIGHT

Back inside the apartment, I had no sooner planted myself on the sofa, deliberating whether or not to bother Colfax with my suspicion of Evan Sandburg, when my cell phone rang again. There was no number displayed.

"Now what?" I muttered, answering it.

"Dave, this is Marnie," the voice said. "You told me to call if anything else happened."

"What's happened?"

"We got another letter. This one came to the office. It's a ransom note."

"Exactly what does it say?"

"It says, 'We have him. Instructions will follow.'"

"That's it?"

"That's it, but it looks exactly like the other letters. What should I do?"

"I really think it's time to talk to the police," I told her.

"I don't want to do that."

"Marnie, you might not have a choice anymore."

"What does that mean?"

"Annemarie has been murdered. Her body was found under the Malibu pier. The police will likely be contacting the house wanting to speak with Vince whether you like it or not."

"Murdered? How?"

"Strangled."

"My god. Do the kids know?"

"I have no idea. I'm assuming the police will contact them."

"Maybe I should first."

"I'd wait. Let the police handle it."

"Did one of her druggie friends kill her?"

"They don't know who did it. I was simply called and informed about the discovery of her body."

"The police called you?"

"The detective in charge, Dane Colfax, recognized the name Mazetta. He's the one who interviewed Vince about Palmer Hanley's death a while back, and also the friend in the department I mentioned."

"Does he know Vince is missing?"

"No, I kept Vince's name out of it. But if Colfax can't locate him in the wake of Annemarie's murder...well, I shouldn't speculate."

It wasn't necessary anyway; she did it for me. "He'll assume Vince is the killer and that's why he vanished," Marnie said.

"Which is why you should report Vince's disappearance and those letters to the cops."

"Why won't you accept the fact that he was abducted?"

"Well, in light of this ransom note, it's pretty hard not to. But showing everything to the police will enable them to clear Vince of murdering Annemarie."

"Unless they theorize that Vince created those letters himself and arranged to have them delivered here, to set up his alibi and explain his absence while he goes off and kills her."

"I thought you said Vince wasn't capable of murder."

"I just don't know what to think anymore. I'm at my wit's end, Dave. I can't stay here. I have to go home. Could you swing by this afternoon and look at the note?"

Since we would both be driving in from different directions, we set four o'clock as the meeting time. That would mean I'd have terrible traffic trying to get back through the thick of rush hour, but some things can't be helped.

"Now what?" Hannah asked after I set the phone down.

"A ransom letter for Vince Mazetta," I said. "At least the prologue to a ransom letter. Vince's wife wants me come by to examine it."

"Do you need me to go with you again?"

"No, you can stay here. Basically all I can do is examine this new letter and try to convince her to turn everything over to the police."

"Why doesn't she want to?"

"That's a good question, isn't it? I don't know if there's something about Vince she feels she has to hide, but whatever her reason she's adamant about it."

While waiting to hit the road again, I pulled out the earlier letters and re-examined them. I don't know what I expected to find this time, but whatever it was, it wasn't there.

"Do you need to call Copper back?" Hannah asked.

Copper was her pet name for Dane Colfax, who replied in kind by calling her *Red*. The two had established an easy rapport, which was great, as long as it didn't become too easy.

Okay, so maybe having finally found my soul mate, I'm a teeny bit jealous of her chemistry with one of my friends.

"I'm going to hold off on contacting Dane again," I said. "I'd thought about it after making the scarf connection, but now there's a possible connection between the murder and Vince himself which I don't want to reveal to the police. Turning in your own client isn't the sort of thing that generates good user reviews on Yelp."

"But that won't matter since this is your last case."

"Y-es, but…it's still the principle of the thing."

"Okay, I'll trust you."

I decided to head out to meet Marnie a little early which was good since traffic was murder (so to speak). It took more than an hour to fight my way to the Benedict Canyon mansion. I was expecting to see Philly waiting for me at the gate, but he was nowhere to be found. When I rang the bell, it was Marnie's voice that came over the intercom.

"Hi, Dave, come on in," she said.

By the time the gate opened and I drove up and parked, she was waiting at the door, dressed in a loose green blouse and dark gray slacks, and her hair was down. I could not place the role she was playing; maybe this was the paper doll version of Marnie before the various costumes were donned.

"I only got in a few minutes ago myself," she said, leading me inside.

"No Philly tonight?" I asked.

"I sent him on an errand at the plant, and then called the office and asked that they keep him busy for at least an hour. Philly's an asset in his own mountainous way, but his constant hovering is getting on my nerves."

Once in the living room, I eased onto the sofa. "Has Philly ever shown violent tendencies?"

"You mean…is he a leg-breaker?"

"Something like that."

"I daresay he's scared the hell out of a few people over the years, but I've never known him to actually harm anyone. If Vince were threatened by someone with a gun, Philly would be more likely to step in front of him and take the bullet himself than fire back at the shooter."

"He's really that dedicated?"

"To Vince, he is. Someone should establish the Philip Lepkowitz Award for Unwavering Loyalty, though I'm not sure who else would qualify."

"Lepkowitz?"

Marnie smiled. "I'll bet you thought he was Italian."

"It had crossed my mind."

"That's what adhering to stereotypes gets you."

I made a mental note to write that down later in the notepad I carry to accommodate such revelations. For now I thought it best to keep my mind on business.

"Can I see the new letter?" I asked.

"Of course." She picked it up from a table and handed it to me. She was right. Except for the content, it was identical to the others.

WE have him. Instructions will follow.

"I wonder why the word WE is in capitals?" I mused.

"I figured it meant there was more than one person involved in the plot."

"Right, but no other word in the letter is rendered in all caps, and since these notes were made on a computer, it can't be dismissed as the only newspaper or magazine option for those two particular letters. This word must have additional meaning. Maybe it's telling us we're not simply dealing with two or more individuals, but rather a group or organization."

"You mean like the mob," Marnie said.

"I don't know. But let me stress once again that I really think you should—"

"Go to the police, I know. God, I really don't want to."

"Has Vince had trouble with the police in the past?"

"What makes you ask that?"

"Your reluctance to get them involved. I know Vince didn't like being questioned by my detective friend during that previous case, but your reaction goes beyond even that. So far you've adamantly refused to call the cops. That has to come from somewhere."

She took a long time before saying, "This is for your ears only, Dave, and I mean it. It's not about Vince. He does have a dislike of policemen that goes back to when he and Annemarie were still married. She was arrested a time or two for possession, and the cops were, shall we say, less than respectful. He told me they were downright rude and insulting. Outside of that, he has no history with the LAPD. But I do."

Uh oh. I wasn't sure I wanted to know what, but since I'm the one banging on the door, it had to open.

"I was involved in something a few years ago that I do not want the authorities to remember," she went on, rising and starting to pace across the living room. "And before your mind automatically goes there, no, I was not a prostitute."

"Um, I wouldn't have presumed you were," I said, weakly.

"Maybe not, but when a woman who doesn't look like a regular from *American Horror Story* confesses to having a past she doesn't want revealed, that's the logical assumption. Before I met Vince, I operated my own company. I offered wealth management strategies to downsized executives with 401ks. Some of my strategies were risky. My clients knew that going in. But when the global financial crisis hit, they seemed to forget all the fine print and demanded their investments back. The problem was by then the money was gone. For a while I tried robbing Peter to pay Paul, but couldn't maintain it."

"You were operating a Ponzi scheme?" I asked.

She frowned. "I don't like that word. And I never set out to cheat my clients. It's just that things happened, and…"

"You got caught."

"No, I didn't."

"You didn't?"

"Dave, most rich men don't listen to women about anything, let alone how to invest their money. That's why the big companies are not called Charlotte Schwab or Edwina Jones. So I invented a fictitious male owner to front the business, and everything was fine at first. No matter what they say in the commercials, people really don't want to meet face-to-face with their investment counselors. They just want to know that their money is being handled for maximum return. Then the crap hit the fan and I decided to have Victor Ludorum…that was my fictitious financial genius…suddenly up and run out, taking the money with him. Interpol is still looking for him."

"Victor Ludorum," I repeated, "that sounds faintly familiar."

"It's Latin for 'winner of the games.' But even the church doesn't use Latin anymore, so it was a pretty safe name to hide behind. Anyway, I professed my innocence to every client, every investigator, the police, the FBI, and anyone else who showed up wanting to know where Victor Ludorum was. I managed to avoid being named in the class action suit against good old Victor by disclosing that I had no money, which was true. I lost as much in the crash as my clients did. Eventually the authorities decided to believe me and stopped harassing me. But if I were to show up again with a story about my husband having vanished just like Victor Ludorum did… well, I'm sure at least one of them would get out a pencil and start playing connect-a-dot."

"What are you going to do when they show up about Annemarie?"

"I was hoping you could suggest something."

"I can't advise you to break the law."

"I don't want to break the law."

I thought for a few moments and then said, "Your company went under before you met Vince, right?"

Marnie nodded.

"What was your name then?"

"My real first name is Margaret. My maiden name is Calloway."

"So back then the police, the FBI, and everybody knew you as Margaret Calloway."

"Maggie Calloway. I went by Maggie. I still go by Marnie Calloway at the office."

"Okay. When you talk to the police, don't tell them your original name."

"Won't they look it up?" she asked.

"Only if you give them reason to. Just present yourself as Marnie Mazetta, Vince's wife, which is who the police will be expecting if they come here. Out of curiosity, what did you look like when you had your financial service company?"

"A little younger, obviously."

"Have you changed your hair color?"

"I've lightened it. And I was a bit heavier then. And I wore glasses, too. Now I use contacts. Now that I think about it, I used to have a little mole in my cheek, too. Vince asked me to get it removed. I guess that's one dot that can't be connected."

"With a different appearance and a different name, I wouldn't waste too much time worrying," I told her.

"You can't guarantee they won't find out, though."

"Marnie, I can't really guarantee anything."

"God," she sighed. "I'd better consult a lawyer, hadn't I?"

"Does Vince have one on retainer?"

"Sure, but Lester mostly handles business matters, not personal ones. Besides, I couldn't tell Lester everything I've told you. It would get back to Vince."

"You mean even *he* doesn't know about the whole Victor Ludorum thing?'

"Why would I tell him?" she cried. "Since the business wiped me out along with my clients, I had to go to work to keep eating. I got a job at Perfect Friends as a secretary in the marketing department. I barely even saw Vince back then. One day I was drafted to take notes from him for a speech he was scheduled to give to some professional organization or other, and something clicked between the two of us. Before long I was working directly for him. A year later we were married. I didn't say anything because I didn't want to start the marriage with past baggage. What I really didn't want was for any of my former clients to find out my new husband was owner of a successful, lucrative business and was living in a mansion in the hills. Even though Vince had nothing whatsoever to do with Victor Ludorum, a few of those bastards would have tried to recoup their losses off of his back, and all you need is one crazy judge to approve a frivolous lawsuit."

"I have to ask this, Marnie. Do you think Vince's kidnapping has anything to do with your previous activities?"

I was steeling myself for her to get angry, but instead she deflated. Lowering her head, she floated to a chair and sank into it. "I've asked myself the same question a hundred times over the last couple days. What if somebody didn't bother with the courts? What if they found out who I was and whose wife I am and this is their way of trying to get their money back?"

And if it was a consortium of former clients working together, that would explain the emphasis on *WE* in the notes.

I kept that tidbit to myself.

"When we discover who's behind, this we can ask," I said. "Until then, I'd like to take this letter."

"Yes, take it before Philly sees it. And since you asked us to save the envelopes…"

She got up and walked over to a table, where she picked one up and carried it over to me.

There was, of course, no return address and the mailing address was put on by a printer. It showed the Perfect Friends address, with *Attn: Marnie*

"You said this arrived at the office?" I asked.

"Yes. Is that important?"

I took a moment to think.

Don't hurt yourself, Robert Mitchum said inside my head.

"Shut up, Mitch," I muttered under my breath, not realizing at first I was speaking aloud.

"What?" Marnie asked.

"Oh, nothing. Sorry. I'm wondering why the sender of this letter used only your first name."

"Maybe they didn't know my last name," she offered. "Maybe they only knew I was Vince's assistant. But wouldn't that mean…"

"I think it means the kidnapper knows you're Vince's wife," I said. "That's why letters have arrived both here at home and at the plant."

"What should I do?"

"The hardest possible thing to do in a situation like this…nothing. Just wait for the next letter, the one that will reveal the actual ransom demand. I'm sorry, but that's all you can do. Meanwhile, I'll keep working on this and hope for a lead."

Just as I was rising to leave, my cell phone rang.

It was my home land-line number that appeared on the screen.

"Hannah?" I answered.

"Dave, he's had another attack," she replied.

"Dad?"

"Yes. Ma Beauchamp just called. They're taking him back to Cedars. I'm on my way there myself."

"Oh, lord," I moaned.

"This one sounds bad, Dave. You need to get there as soon as you can."

NINE

Hannah and Mom were in the ER waiting room when I arrived. I went to Mom to hug her and she all but collapsed in my arms. I eased her back into one of the incongruously stylish chairs.

"It'll be okay," I said.

"Will it?" she moaned.

Turning to Hannah, I asked if there was any news.

"They took him upstairs about forty-five minutes ago," she said. "That's all I know. Ma Beauchamp said he was fine today until he wasn't."

Turning back to Mom I asked, "Was there any trigger for the attack?"

"What?"

"Was he doing anything in particular that might have overtaxed him? Lifting something, maybe?"

"No. He went to the bathroom and then didn't come out. After a while, I went to check. He was lying on the floor. God…why did these quack doctors let him go in the first place?"

"They did what they thought was best," I said, sitting beside her.

We sat and said little more until I went to the gift shop and bought a newspaper, bringing it back so we could argue over who wanted what section first. It turns out I was wrong: Mom requested the crossword puzzle, Hannah the California section, while I kept the front section.

After twenty or so minutes, a doctor appeared. At least he was dressed like a doctor. The guy in the white coat looked to be about nineteen.

"Mrs. Beauchamp, I'm Dr. Metcalf," he said

"Doctor?" she cried, rising. "You can't be old enough!"

"I assure you I'm a practicing cardiologist."

"Well, practice on someone else. I demand a real doctor."

"Mom, chill," I said, which surprised her. I rose and extended my hand. "I'm Dave Beauchamp, Carl's son, and this is my fiancée Hannah Skaal. What's happening with my dad?"

"I'm not going to sugar coat it, Mr. Beauchamp. We're a bit beyond the take-it-easy-and-watch-your-diet phase. We're continuing to run tests but I believe we're looking at a bypass operation."

"Oh, my god," Mom moaned. "I knew it."

"Such operations have very high success rates," Dr. Metcalf said.

"When will the operation take place?" I asked.

"As I said, we're still testing so I can't give you a definite answer on that yet. We should know more this evening. Until then there's not a lot for you to do but wait."

"Can I go see him?" Mom begged.

"I'm sorry, not yet."

"What if I never see him again?"

"Don't say things like that," Hannah said gently, placing a hand on her shoulder.

"Will you be doing the procedure?" I inquired.

"With others, but yes."

"Have you ever done heart surgery before?" Mom asked.

Metcalf smiled and narrowed his eyes, but it was not an expression of humor so much as annoyed resignation. "Believe it or not, I get this all the time. Yes, I have done this procedure before. I am thirty-four years old and I've been a heart surgeon for three years. I've had many patients."

I fully sympathized with the doctor, being in the same boat: looking far too young to be taken for real. Maybe that was why I was seriously losing patience when Mom kept it up.

"You look like a child!" she prattled. "Doctors aren't supposed to look like children. They're supposed to look like they know what they're doing. I will not consent to any operation until I see a real doctor!"

"Mrs. Beauchamp, I know this is a stressful situation," Dr. Metcalf began, but Mom wouldn't let him finish."

"Oh, you *know*, do you?" she cried. "What do you know? What you learned last week in tenth grade?"

"Mom, this is not the time to play I'm-the-only-one-who-knows-anything," I said.

She turned and glared at me, her stare dropping the temperature of the room by twenty degrees. "Oh, of course *you'd* take his side! You never had the sense God gave a mosquito! If you had, you wouldn't waste your life impersonating a policeman, as though you're dressing up as a detective for Halloween."

Let the record show that this was the moment I finally snapped.

"*Mom, shut up!*" I roared, silencing the entire waiting room. "This isn't about you, all right? It's not about you being the only person on the planet blessed with intelligence and common sense! It's about Dad and what he's about to go through, and if you can't contribute anything useful, then sit down and let the human beings in the room deal with it!"

Both Mom and Hannah stared back at me, aghast, while Dr. Metcalf stiffened.

"I have to get back now," he said, practically running away from us.

"David Randolph Beauchamp!" Mom cried. "You...you..."

"I what, Mom?"

"You're not allowed to speak to me like that."

"Oh, I'm not allowed? Well, I've had it with your constant criticism. My entire life! Nothing's ever good enough for you. You have to find fault no matter what!"

"We're all stressed, Dave," Hannah said, reaching out and petting my arm in an attempt to calm me down.

It didn't work.

"You think I wanted to be a lawyer?" I went on, oblivious to anyone else watching and listening. "I got a law degree because you insisted that I follow in Dad's footsteps. I was terrible at it and I hated it. Now you don't like it that I'm a private detective. Well, you know what? Tough! You had your life, and I've got mine."

"We put you through Whittier Law School!" she snapped back. "If you don't like your degree then you can pay the money back."

"I'll write you a check."

"I don't know why you're saying these things."

"I know you don't. Awareness has never been part of your skill set."

She opened her mouth to speak again but I didn't wait for it. Instead I turned away from her and marched to another row of chairs, dropping into one.

Of course, as soon as I took a breath I felt like the worst human being in the world. I stared at the floor. Hannah sat beside me and put her head on my shoulder.

Mom finally sat down four seats away. After a couple minutes, during which I was probably supposed to be the one to apologize, she said, "I really don't care if you're not a lawyer. I just hate that you put yourself into danger all the time, is all."

"I can appreciate that," I replied, quietly. "But I have to be responsible for my own life, which includes making my own mistakes. And believe it or not, I'm acutely aware when I've done so. I don't need to have them pointed out."

The gag order goes for you too, Mitchum! I thought furiously.

He must have gotten the message because he said nothing.

"You've made me feel like a horrible mother."

I could have responded in any number of different ways, but all I said was, "Sorry, that wasn't my intent."

"What was your intent, then? Humiliation?"

"You mean humiliation like telling the doctor in charge of saving my father's life that I'm an idiot?"

"I...I...ohhh."

Nothing more was spoken for several more minutes. Then Hannah—who somehow instinctively knows how to make things better—said, "Well, I'm new here, but I love you both. So, if you stop talking to each other, I guess I'll have to carry messages between you."

I was the first to chuckle, then Mom started in.

"Rotten kid," she said, still chuckling.

"Mom, I'm thirty-three. I think that makes me a rotten adult. You know, it's really Dad we need to be concerned with now."

"I completely agree," Mom said. "That's all I ever wanted. That's why I insisted on a more official-looking doctor."

"I know. I was a little startled at first, too, but this isn't Sandbox General Hospital. It's Cedars. They know what they're doing. Can I get anything for you? Coffee? Water?"

"I think I'm capable of getting my own..." Mom's voice trailed off, and then she sighed. "My lord, you've actually caused me to listen to myself. I'm fine, Dave, but thank you for asking."

"No problem at all," I said.

"We sure scared the snot out of everybody else, didn't we?" She seemed almost proud of making an impact.

"Yes, we did, Mom," I said with a laugh. "Look, if it's okay with you, I'd like to step outside for a few minutes and clear my head."

"You don't have to ask me, you know."

"I'll go, too," Hannah interjected, and the two of us went out to the ER parking lot.

Once the automatic doors closed behind us, I said, "Hannah, you must think I'm a horrible person, but I've had that bottled up for years. It just... erupted."

"Your mom's upset too, you know," Hannah said.

"I know. It has to be tough on her. But I also know from experience that this is how she deals with upset, by finding fault with everybody else as deflection. Growing up I didn't have any siblings to share the abuse with. I got it all."

"You know how much I love you, Dave, but I'm not sure you know what abuse really is," Hannah said. "I've never told you about mine."

"From the Temple?"

"No. From my family."

Having just witnessed my explosion in a baggage factory, I wasn't sure this was the right moment for Hannah to unload on her upbringing. But I held my tongue.

I can sometimes.

We walked to a nearby concrete bench and sat down.

"My parents, "Hannah began, "they didn't really want me in the first place. I've heard other people say that but mine really did not. I ruined their lives and they never let me forget it. They were only sixteen when I was born, which meant they were forced to throw away whatever plans they'd had for life and deal with me."

"They had a little bit to do with that situation, too, I'd think."

"Well, sure. But when Dad wasn't around Mom would blame him for everything, and I'm pretty sure Dad blamed her as well, but he didn't talk about it as much. As time went on, they both found it easier to blame me for being born."

"What sort of plans were they forced to abandon?"

"I don't think they even knew. All they knew is that they didn't want to be high school freshmen and parents at the same time. I think they were bitter about having to get married, too, but my Dad's folks told him that was the only honorable thing to do."

"What did your mom's parents say?"

She shrugged. "Mom was an exchange student from Sweden. I never met her parents. They were probably mad at her because in Sweden they teach kids about sex when they're really young, and that's supposed to cut down on unwanted pregnancies."

"Your dad is Swedish too, isn't he? I mean, your name being Skaal, and all."

"Skaal is actually Danish, but Dad might have told her he was Swedish to get into bed with her. My mom was really gorgeous when she was young. I think a lot of guys wanted to date her."

"Speaking for purely selfish reasons, I'm glad they chose not to end the pregnancy."

"Oh, that was out of the question. My American grandparents are ultra-Catholic. They didn't consider giving me up for adoption, either, though I wish they had. It would have made for a happier childhood."

"Jeez. Where did you grow up?"

"Gardena."

"No, I mean in a house? An apartment?"

"Oh. Well, my mom had been living with a host family while she was an exchange student, but they hadn't bargained on a baby. So she moved in with my dad's folks. Mom tried to return to high school after I was born but my grandmother told her she had to stay home and deal with me. Then she got pregnant again, with my brother Christian."

"Wait, why did your mom have another baby if taking care of you was such a burden for her?"

Hannah smiled sadly. "It sounds weird, doesn't it? The story that I was told…over and over…was that I was a horrible child, always crying and screaming so much that everybody wanted to kill me. My grandfather… Dad's dad…was getting so sick of me that he threatened to move out of the house himself. So everyone decided that Mom's folks had to get involved, even if it was only to send money from Sweden so we could all move out and get a place of our own. But Mormor and Farfar didn't like the fact that I'd been conceived before they were married, and thought giving us any money was rewarding bad behavior. So, Mom and Dad got the idea that, if they had another baby, this one legitimate, maybe Mormor and Farfar could be convinced to help out."

"What a reason to have a kid."

"Yeah, but it worked. I was nearly two when Chris was born and he proved to be the perfect child. He didn't cry or scream when he was a baby. He never had an earache. Growing up, everything he ever did was right, and everything I ever did was wrong."

"I'm sorry."

"It's not your fault, Dave."

"I know, but I'm still sorry because it wasn't your fault, either."

"Yeah. But you can't change the past. Things got a little better after Dad found an apartment that was big enough for the four of us, at least physically. He got a job, which meant more money. But it also meant Mom, Christian, and I, were home alone all day. Before long I became more of a servant to Chris than a sister. One time my mom said I wasn't really part of the family because of my red hair. Everyone else is blond. That was her way of turning me into live-in help."

"How did you survive an environment like that?"

"Well, you already know some of it. I started smoking pot when I was thirteen, and that made it seem like things were easier. I also had a good friend in middle school that I spent as much time with as I could. We kind of got into trouble sometimes, but at least she liked me. When the point came where Christian was criticizing and dissing me as much as my folks, I decided I'd had it and ran away. I asked my friend if I could stay at her house, which was fine for a while because her parents felt sorry for me. But then they got tired of me, too. I told you we got into a little trouble…we did some shoplifting…and Sheila's parents blamed me for that, telling her I was a bad influence. Sheila's mom called mine and said that she had to come and get me, but Mom refused. She told them to just kick me out when they were tired of me."

"Jeez."

"Anyway, I wrote to Mormor and Farfar and tried to explain the situation, and begged them to send some money, which they did…in krones. I guess they thought that was funny or else they thought I'd never be able to figure out how to exchange it for dollars. But I did, and with that little bit of money, I was able to leave Sheila's house and try to live on my own. That's when I dropped out of school. You know how well all that worked. I ended up getting sucked into the...the place, but at least I got off drugs and learned some skills. And, of course, I met Mr. Hanley."

For the first time I realized that Hannah might actually be the Temple of Theotologics' only actual success story.

She put her arms around me. "Then a handsome prince came and rescued me, and here I am."

"Do you ever see your folks anymore?"

She shook her head. "I'm not even sure they're still together. By the time I left home, Dad had started to drink, and he wasn't a very nice drunk."

"He didn't abuse you, did he?"

"You mean mess with me? No. Why would he? Mom was still gorgeous. Besides, that's pretty sick, messing with your own daughter. No, he just yelled a lot and said really hurtful things. I haven't seen Christian since I ran away either, though something funny happened after that newspaper story came out, the one about the collapse of the...the place that mentioned me by name. He read the story and then tracked me down."

"Hannah, you never told me that."

"There wasn't much to tell. He's some big lawyer now and he's going to run for a political office, and he didn't want anyone to know that his sister was a former user who was caught up in a scandal. His letter included a check for five-thousand as payment in return for my never trying to get in touch with him. That's the part that's funny."

"Why?"

"Because he thinks five-thousand dollars is more money than I'll ever see at one time in my life. He doesn't know I'm about to become a millionaire."

"I hope you didn't tell him."

"I didn't respond at all. I thought about tearing the check up and mailing it back to him, but then I decided to donate it to the Palmer Hanley Foundation once it gets up and running."

After hearing all this, my familial problems seemed pretty miniscule, and I told her as much.

"Well, I know what it's like when you think your own mother doesn't like you," she said, "but I don't think Ma Beauchamp wants to make you upset. Maybe something happened in her life that she doesn't want you to know about and that's what makes her defensive."

"Have you ever thought of studying to be a professional psychologist?" I asked.

"I used to think about it but I couldn't say it out loud when I was inside. Part of the place's philosophy was that psychiatry was evil. You couldn't even say the word unless it was to trash it."

We sat outside for a few more minutes, and then grew tired of the exhaust from all the cars driving up and returned to the waiting room.

Mom was up and pacing when we approached.

"I suppose you two were talking about me out there," she said.

"As a matter of fact, we were," I told her.

"I did the best I could for you, Dave."

"I know you did, Mom, and I love you for it. And getting all that off my chest makes me feel lighter and at the same time guilty as heck for hurting you. But it's gone now, and I don't think it's going to come back. So how about giving your rotten kid a hug?"

She grabbed me then and actually started crying. I let her.

When she was done, she sat back down, wiped her eyes, and said, "Can we talk about your father now?"

"Of course."

"Kids, I don't think I can take care of him once he comes home," she said. "I'm not young."

"You're only fifty-nine, Mom," I said.

"Dave, I have something to confess. You might as well hear this too, Hannah. I've lied about my age my entire married life. I'm not fifty-nine. I'll be seventy next year."

"You're...*sixty-nine*?"

She nodded. "Your father knows, of course, but I never admitted it to anyone else. What do they call women like me today? Cougars?"

"Mom, I'm not sure a difference of five years makes you a cougar. Though now I understand where I get my trait of looking so much younger."

She flashed a grin and said, "Flatterer. My point is that turning sixty was easy, particularly when people thought I was only in my forties. But seventy is different. I get tired much more easily now. Dealing with your father would be like taking care of a dependent child and I'm not sure I'm up for that."

"I can help," Hannah said. "I mean, it's what I've done for the last several years."

"Oh, dear, I couldn't ask you to do that."

"You're not asking. I'm volunteering."

Over Mom's shoulder I could see Dr. Metcalf heading toward us.

"Hi, again, folks," he called out. "Are we...all okay?"

"Never better," I said, meaning it.

"I'm glad to hear that. I've got some good news, followed by some not-so-good news. Carl has been stabilized and is out of immediate danger. The not-so-good news is that he needs some help breathing. He's hooked up to a respirator and is sleeping right now. If everything goes as expected, he might be up for a visit tomorrow. Until then you should all go home and try to get some rest. I promise you Carl is enjoying the best care possible."

"Young man," Mom said, "I've known Carl Beauchamp for thirty-six years. He might be *getting* the best care possible, but I seriously doubt he's *enjoying* it."

"Well, you've got me there," the doctor said with a chuckle. "I should have said he is *receiving* the best care possible. We will be in touch if anything happens, but I'm more encouraged now than I was earlier."

After he left, I turned to Mom and asked, "Will you be okay going home?"

"I'm certainly not going to stay in this lobby," she replied.

"I mean, do you need me to come home with you?"

"I don't know, Dave. I don't know."

"How about if I go home with you?" Hannah asked.

Mom smiled. "That might be nice."

"Okay. I'll make sure she's taken care of, Dave."

"I have no doubt. I love you, Mom."

Mom and Hannah went off to find her car, while I hung around in the lobby to make sure they were able to. When they didn't come back after twenty minutes, I took it as a good sign.

Driving home I rationalized that Dad was getting the best of care, and so was Mom, thanks to Hannah.

But where was I? Stuck in a ridiculous case with no real leads that the police should be handling entirely.

Once it was over I vowed to retire from the PI game.

It's not like anyone will notice, a voice said inside my head. Welcome back, Mitch.

When I got back to my empty, very quiet apartment I noticed the message light on my phone blinking. "God, I hope it's only good news," I uttered, punching the play button.

Dave, it's Vince Mazetta.

It was his voice, but now it bore an alien tone of fear and distress.

They...they got Annemarie. Now they're coming for me.

"Vince, who is they?" I asked redundantly, since it was a recording.

They know...they know...

"They know *what*?"

Aw, shit...they're here...

The call cut off.

I tried to be alarmed, but didn't have the energy. Instead I staggered into the bedroom and dropped my clothes on the floor before falling into the bed. Even without Hannah's warm, comforting presence, and with the panic-stricken voice of Vince Mazetta still ringing between my ears, physical and emotional exhaustion won the day and I somehow managed to fall asleep that night. Maybe it was the only thing I could actually do, since every other part of my life had spun completely out of my control.

TEN

I woke up as the morning light seeped through the window.

Only a few remnants of my nightmare remained with me, though it was a beaut.

I was a defendant in a courtroom…a black-and-white courtroom with heavy, highly contrasted shadows and diagonal lines on the walls that appeared to come from nowhere.

I was being questioned by my mother.

"Isn't it true," she said, "that you are, and always have been, a rotten kid?"

"Am I under oath?" I asked.

"Of course."

"Then…"

"Your honor, I object to the question," the defense attorney shouted.

It was Elvis.

"Withdrawn," Mom said. "Let me ask this, then. Isn't it true that you are responsible for the death of your father?"

"My father's not dead."

"How can you be so certain?"

"Because…well…I can't, but—"

"I rest my case."

Mom went and sat down behind the prosecution table and started doing a crossword.

Then Elvis got up. "C'mon, man, you had nothing to do with the death of that crazy woman, right?"

"Which crazy woman?" I asked, looking at Mom.

I heard a collective gasp from the jury box. When I looked over I saw the jury was comprised of twelve different actresses, including Kim Novak, Katherine Hepburn, Rita Hayworth, and Veronica Lake.

They were all Marnie Mazetta underneath.

"Did you or did you not strangle that woman under the pier?" Elvis demanded.

"I did not. Did you?"

"Whoa, man, I'll ask the questions here. Your Honor, I ask permission to treat this loser as a hostile witness."

"Permission granted," the judge said, and for the first time I looked up to see her.

It was Hannah.

"Hostile, insulting, and negligent," she added. "Everybody around you dies, and you're mean to your mother. And you're getting weird. Ghosts live in your head." Then leaning toward me, she delivered the knockout blow. "I don't think I love you anymore."

Just then my dream-self remembered that I *had* murdered Annemarie and left her body buried in the sand; a poisonous cocktail of guilt and terror completely overtook me.

The film broke and my eyes snapped open.

I was panting.

Looking at the clock I saw it was a little after six in the morning; too early to call Mom and apologize again.

Jumping out of bed, I ran out to check my phone. There was no flashing light, which means nobody called and left a message, including the hospital to tell me things had taken a turn for the worse.

Jeez…why do I beat myself up so much?

I can't speak for you, Robert Mitchum chimed in, *but for me it's a lot of fun.*

"Just a dream and now it's over," I murmured. "You're fine, Mom's coping, Dad's still alive, and Hannah still loves you. It's only inside your head."

Vince Mazetta's problem wasn't though.

Pressing the phone's playback button, I listened to his old message hoping it might sound different in the morning light of a new day.

No such luck. The urgency was still in the voice as was the fear, and it still ended with, '*Aw, shit…they're here…*' But now it sounded hollow like he was speaking from an unnatural position that affected his voice. Curled up inside a car trunk, maybe?

Can you even get cell service inside a car trunk?

I thought about calling Marnie Mazetta to see if she had also received a call from Vince, but then decided against it. Aside from the early hour, if she had spent the night waiting by the phone, and then the call turned out to be me and not the kidnappers (or whoever was behind this), it would only drive her further into a fetal position.

You can *get cell service in a fetal position*, Bob Hope cracked inside my head.

It was nearly eight and I was halfway through a bowl of Trader Joe's Honey-O's when the phone finally rang, and I grabbed it before swallowing. "Dave Bchhrhhmmm," I said through the cereal.

There was a pause before Hannah's voice said, "Are you okay?"

"Yes, I just have a mouthful of cereal," I told her.

"I wanted to let you know that things here are all right. Your mom was up until real late, talking. She finally went to bed about two or so. I think it helped her, talking like that. Have you called the hospital?"

"Not yet," I said.

"I did, and they said that your dad is in stable condition."

"Good. Did you get any sleep?"

"About five hours, but I'm okay. I expect Ma Beauchamp to stay in bed for several more hours, so I'll rest a little more."

"Do I need to come over?"

"Not right now. There's nothing you could do."

"Why don't you call me back when Mom's up and I'll swing by then," I said. "We can figure out the battle plan. Tell her not to worry about fixing dinner. I'll force her to go to a restaurant."

"I love you," she said, and I really needed to hear that after my horrific dream.

"I love you, too."

After hanging up, I punched the playback button again and listened to Vince Mazetta's message one more time, paying close attention to any noise in the background that might have offered a clue as to where he was.

There was nothing, of course, no other sound. That only worked in movies. Pulling a writing pad out of my desk drawer, I made some notes, jotting down the word *they* for starters.

Who were *they*?

After that I wrote *They got Annemarie*, and underlined the word *got*. Not they *caught*, or they *found*, or even they *killed*, but they *got* her. Was there significance to that? If this were a war movie, *got* would indicate that the enemy had picked off the best of our boys, leading to the clichéd battle cry, *They got Johnnie!* But this wasn't a war movie.

Unless…

Could it be that Vince's disappearance and Annemarie's death were part of a mob turf war?

Looking at the sentence again, I finally realized the question I should have asked first thing: how did Vince find out Annemarie was dead? To my knowledge it had not been reported anywhere, which limited the sources to Detective Dane Colfax, Marnie Mazetta, and me. And I was the one who told Marnie. But how could Colfax or anyone else in the police tell Vince if he's being held? The same was true for Marnie…unless Marnie really did know where he was and was faking the distraught wife routine. What about Philly? Had Marnie told him? If so, could he know where Vince is?

Your math's a little off, kid, Bogie said inside my head. *You've left out one person.*

"No," I said aloud, "no one else knew Annemarie was dead."

What about her killer?

Okay, that made sense. But who *was* her killer?

Hey, finding that out is your job, Bogie replied. *I can't do all the work around here.*

Thanks. So much.

After a leisurely shower and facial massage with an electric shaver (part of being baby-faced is having a thin-to-nonexistent beard), I got dressed and made up my mind to head out. Even though it was Saturday, I decided to swing by the office where I tend to think more clearly for some reason. Being the weekend, there would likely be no one else in the building to distract me as I attempted to formulate a plan of action.

I made it to my building a tad before nine. It was too early for there to be any mail so I went straight to my office on the second floor. Just outside of it, I suddenly froze.

My door was slightly open.

Despite the distractions and stress of the last few days, I knew I had not left it unlocked, let alone ajar.

I slowly pushed the door open and called, "Hello, anyone here?"

No answer.

Entering, I glanced around. It took no time at all to find the object that should not have been there.

Philly Lepkowitz. He was seated in my desk chair.

"Jeez, Philly, you startled me. What are you doing here? And how did you get in?"

He didn't answer.

He couldn't.

The bullet hole in his chest prevented him from talking.

ELEVEN

"Please don't tell me, Beauchamp," Detective Colfax moaned over the phone lines. "*Please* don't tell me!"

"Dane, words cannot express how much I don't want to tell you this, but I have no choice," I replied. "His name is Philly Lepkowitz and he's Vince Mazetta's right hand. *Was* Vince Mazetta's right hand. He's propped up in my office chair with a gunshot wound in his chest."

"It's Saturday and I'm not even supposed to be in today! I came in to finish up some paperwork and the phone rings, and like a dummy I answer it, and guess who's calling with another corpse?"

"Dane, I'm sorry, but there is a dead guy in my office, and I figured I'd better report it rather than not report it."

"You call the locals yet?"

"Not yet."

"I won't bother asking if you shot him because last I heard, you don't carry a gun."

"I still don't."

"Is anyone else's gun lying around?"

"Not that I can see."

"Any signs of forced entry?"

"The door was open, but no, no signs of force. I figure either Philly or his killer picked the lock."

"Los Angeles County covers five-thousand square miles. Why do people keep dumping bodies in your five-hundred feet of it?"

"I wish I knew."

"What was he doing there?"

"I wish I knew that, too. All I can figure is that he came to see me, found a way in, and then someone else came along and shot him…unless he and his killer came to my office together."

"Why would they do that?"

"I don't know, Dane, and I can't ask. Maybe the two of them were looking for something they thought I had here in the office."

"What?"

"I don't know."

"So they search but turn up nothing, and that makes one of them so pissed he shoots the other one?"

"Maybe they thought they'd found something, and once the killer had it, he eliminated Philly and took off."

"I've heard worse," Colfax admitted. "Not much but some. Was your office tossed?"

"No."

"Here's a possibility you're not going to like," Colfax said. "Your friend wants to see you about something and goes to your office, but you're not there. He considers whatever he has to say to you too important for him to simply leave and come back later. So he finds a way inside, lock pick or whatever, and waits. While he does someone else shows up, someone unexpected. Or maybe he was expected, who can say? Whatever the details, Philly is in your chair behind your desk, and someone else shows up. That person reads *Beauchamp Investigations* painted on the door, tries it, and finds it unlocked. He...or she...sees Philly seated behind your desk and shoots."

"But why?'

"That's the part you're not going to like. Because the killer thinks Philly is you. Maybe you were the intended target all along."

Colfax was right; I didn't much care for that theory.

"Nobody would mistake Philly for me," I said. "The guy looked like he was coming to Muhammad."

"Nobody who knows you would. Even if they did, maybe the killer was the shoot-first-look-later type, and as soon as they realized they plugged the wrong guy, they fled."

It was beginning to look like all roads were leading back to the mob. Had a professional hit been put out on me?

"As much as I hate to say it, that could go hand-in-hand with Vince's disappearance," I said.

"Whoa, hold the phone! You're telling me Mazetta is that hypothetical missing person you've been grilling me about?"

Aw, jeez!

"Um, yeah."

"Goddammit, Beauchamp, is there anything *else* you're holding back?"

"No, that was about it. But look, Dane, I've still got a giant economy-sized stiff in my office chair. What should I do about it?"

"Call 911 and wait for your local blues to arrive. Feel free to offer them the theory I've just laid out if it comes up, but don't confuse them with a lot of 'ifs' and 'maybes'. Not yet, anyway."

"All right."

"And whatever you do, stay away from me. I'm too busy to end up dead."

The line cut off.

I looked into the frozen face of Philly Lepkowitz, who was no longer able to look back. "Philly, I wish you could tell me who did this to you," I uttered.

He didn't reply. Not even a shrug.

Those who underplay are the scourge of the theatre, the voice of John Barrymore said inside my head.

I punched 911 into the phone and waited for it to connect.

I reported the murder to the woman who answered and then gave her a brief summary of the details as well as my address.

"Don't go anywhere, sir," she said.

"I don't plan to," I replied, then hung up.

Upon making a closer examination of the office, I found no trace of a gun or bullet. Whoever the killer was took the evidence with him. I sat down in my guest chair and waited for the police to arrive.

Then it hit me.

I carefully opened Philly's suit coat and saw the shoulder holster.

Which was empty.

Either I'm a monkey or Philly was shot with his own gun.

Good job, Cheetah, the voice of Johnny Weissmuller said inside my head.

But that raised another question: if Philly was really as benign as Marnie said, why was he carrying a gun in the first place?

A fleet of cruisers from the North Hollywood division arrived about ten minutes after my call to them, though I don't understand the hurry. Philly wasn't going anywhere.

The first officer on the scene, whose nametag identified him as "Gunn" (seriously), recognized me.

"You're the guy who cracked the murder case with all the old washed-up movie stars, aren't you?"

"Guilty. To *that*, I mean, not this."

More police showed up over the next few minutes, including a fortyish woman in street clothes who identified herself as Detective Belinda Lopez. Her partner, she announced, was trying to find a parking spot.

I could relate.

While waiting, she examined the body including discovering for herself Philly's empty shoulder holster. A few minutes later, a tall blond detective named Benford showed up.

"Did you call for the M.E.?" Lopez asked him.

"He's on his way," Benford replied.

For the next few minutes I recounted the story of finding Philly's body, though I was naturally vague about some of the details of the case.

"Sounds like you're hiding something, Mr. Beauchamp," Benford said.

"I owe my client some confidentiality," I replied. "All I can tell you is that I was investigating on behalf of the man the victim worked for."

"And who would that be?" Lopez asked.

"There is no reason for me to tell you. I am confident you will find his name and maybe even his phone number somewhere on the body."

"Why don't you simply make our job easier by telling us?" Benford asked.

Detective Lopez, meanwhile, was carefully examining Philly's coat pockets. From his breast pocket she pulled out a sheet of paper. "Your address is written on this note, Mr. Beauchamp," she said.

"That would explain why he's here," I replied.

"It's written on what appears to be a page from a company scratch pad. Perfect Friends Pet Food of Cudahy, California. Does that mean anything to you?"

"It does."

"Is that where this guy's employer worked?" Benford asked.

I remained silent.

Then Officer Gunn chimed in. "Wasn't the pet food company involved in that movie star case, too?" he asked. "That's where the horse head came from, right?"

"You can't believe everything you read in the papers," I said.

"The pet food guy's name was Maretta, or Zametta, something like that."

Now Benford was working his smartphone. "Perfect Friends Pet Food, Cudahy, California, Vincent T. Mazetta, CEO," he read. "Is that your client, Mr. Beauchamp?"

"See, your job isn't that hard," I said, smiling.

I did not stress over their learning Vince's name. It was their job, after all, and it was not I who told them, meaning I hadn't broken client confidentiality.

"Can you at least tell us where Mr. Mazetta is?" Detective Lopez asked.

"I cannot. Believe me, I wish I could."

"You didn't shoot this man, did you?" Benford asked.

"Would I have called you if I had?"

"I don't know."

"The answer is no, I did not shoot him. I don't own a gun. If you want to test my hands for powder residue, be my guest."

"You could have worn gloves."

"I had no reason to kill Philly. Even if I had a reason, and somehow acquired a gun, I would not have shot him in my desk chair in my office and then called the police to show him off."

Detective Lopez took over: "Do you have any idea what the victim was doing here, and what his killer was doing here?"

I used that opportunity to repeat Colfax's last theory as though I had thought of it, emphasizing the notion that I might still be in the crosshairs of whoever got Philly. I did not mention my suspicion that he had been shot with his own gun, in part because that contradicted Dane's theory.

"Do you have any idea who would want to kill you?" Lopez asked.

"All I can tell you is that, in the past, people have tried, including one of your own," I said.

"What's that mean?" Benford asked, and I recounted my experiences with a certain LAPD member who moonlit as a professional contract killer.

"Oh, him," Officer Gunn said. "At the academy we were told never to mention his name."

"Then take that advise and be quiet, officer," Detective Lopez snapped.

Another idea came to me at that moment: maybe the killer was a friend or contact of Annemarie Mazetta's who was seeking vengeance for her death? Maybe they thought Philly was involved in it and followed him here, or maybe they thought I was responsible and walked into the office assuming Philly was me.

But heeding Colfax's advice, I kept the additional ifs and maybes to myself.

"Are any of the other tenants of this building in on Saturday?" Lopez asked.

"You can check the offices, but I don't think so. There's a CPA at the end of the hall, but it's not tax season so I doubt he's here."

"No one would have heard the shot then?" Benford pressed.

"Detectives, if you want to go door-to-door to check I'll come with you and introduce you. But if anyone was here, I think they'd probably have revealed themselves by now."

"Unless they were the murderer," Benford went on.

"You think another tenant in this building is the killer?"

"Don't you?"

"To be honest, I hadn't really considered it."

The medical examiner showed up then and began examining the body, pronouncing the approximate time of death between nine and midnight last night.

"Where were you during that time, Mr. Beauchamp?" Benford asked.

"Home alone," I replied. "My dad is in the hospital and I'd been there with my mom and my fiancée. Then I came home."

"But no one can vouch for you between nine and midnight?"

Only my nightmares, I thought. "Look, if you want me to come down to the station and take a polygraph test to prove that I was home all night last night, I'll do it. I'll act as my own counsel."

"You could have paid someone to do the hit for you," Benford added.

"Get a warrant and check my bank account if that makes you happy. I'll write a letter of permission for the judge. Heck, I'd even surrender my passport if I had one."

Note to self: get a passport; now that you're going to have money, it might come in handy.

"I don't think that will be necessary," Lopez said, "at least not at this point. But I'm going to have to kick you out of here for a while now that this is a crime scene. Where can I reach you?"

I fished out a business card and wrote my home number on it before handing it to her. After thanking me, she turned away and began resuming her investigation. I had little choice but to leave my own office.

On the way downstairs I saw two EMTs with a low gurney. I did not stop to say hello.

As I got to the door I pulled out my car keys and dropped them. Nerves, I guess. While I had been grilled by the police before, it had never taken place over a dead body in my office.

Bending down to retrieve the keys, I noticed a crumpled-up piece of paper someone had attempted to lob into the small wastebasket that was by the mailboxes, and missed. I reached for it and was planning to deposit it in the trash, when I noticed there was writing on it. I smoothed out the paper to see what it was.

The paper was lined and appeared to be a page from a small notebook. On one side was written the address to this building and on the other was scrawled, *5/12–SNA TC G19, 10:40a.*

Five-twelve seemed like a date—last Tuesday, in fact—and 10:40 a. was likely a time, ten-forty in the morning.

But what did *SNA TC G19* signify? If it was timing for some kind of snatch, the snatcher needed spellcheck.

I should, of course, have taken this up to Detective Lopez and let her deal with it. But I did not since this slip of paper might also have bearing on the abduction of Vince Mazetta, which was still my case.

I'm glad I've taught you something, kid, Bogie said in my head. Which was great, except that about halfway through the drive home, I realized that if I'd handed it over the police, they could have dusted it for prints and run it through the system to find out *who* had left it.

Said *who* quite possibly being the person who killed Philly.

I'd copy the information from it and hand it over tomorrow, I rationalized.

Then I realized that my prints would be on the paper as well.

"I'll sleep on it," I said aloud.

My apartment was just as empty and quiet as when I'd left it, at least until the phone rang. Assuming it was Mom or Hannah, I grabbed it.

It wasn't either. It was somebody pressing the code button out front.

I nearly dropped the phone when I recognized the voice.

"Did you hear what I said?" he repeated. "Open the damned door and let me in!"

"I'll be right there," I told Vince Mazetta.

TWELVE

When I got to the lobby and opened the front door to let Vince in, it took a minute to find him. He was crouching behind a bush.

"Vince, what are you doing?" I asked.

"Trying to stay alive," he said before dashing into the building.

On the way to my apartment he said, "It took you long enough to open the door."

"I don't live in the lobby, Vince," I told him. "And it wasn't that long. Plus I was a little surprised to hear from you. I am glad you got away, though."

"You mean from the guy who was following me?"

"I mean from the people who had abducted you."

"Abducted? What the hell are you talking about?"

"You mean you weren't…okay, come on in. We need to talk."

Stepping inside the apartment, Vince said, "Is anyone else here?"

"No. My fiancée is with my mother."

"Good move."

He plopped down on my sofa and visibly relaxed. "Christ, what a day," he uttered.

Sitting on the other side of the sofa, I began, "Okay, first things first… you're saying you were not abducted or kidnapped?"

"Of course I wasn't. You thought I was?"

"Yes, and so does your wife."

"Oh. So you figured out that me and Marnie aren't just boss and employee?"

"Well, it wasn't actually figuring it out as much as her telling me so. I recommended she go to the police but she didn't want to. It hardly matters now since they know anyway."

"Oh, for…I suppose you reported it to them?"

"You don't know what's happened, do you?"

"What I don't know is what the hell you're talking about. If you have something to say, come out and say it."

"Annemarie has been murdered."

"Holy shit."

"So has Philly."

On that he leapt up off the sofa. "*What*?" he cried. "How? When?"

"With a gun and in my office."

"In your…"

"And Annemarie was found a few days ago on the beach under the Malibu Pier."

Vince opened his mouth but no sound came out. He sank back down on the sofa. "Holy Mother of God," he finally said. "I thought maybe this time she was going to make it. That's why I sent her to that expensive place by the ocean. All that money paid out to that quack in charge, Wyatt Earp—"

"Wyatt Worsley," I corrected.

"If you say so. Might as well have been Wyatt Earp, since she ended up dead instead of cured. Jesus, what kind of sadistic parent would name their kid *Wyatt Worsley*? Poor bastard's life must have been hell in school. You got anything to drink around here, Beauchamp?"

"I'm not much of a drinker, but there might be some wine."

"Red?"

I went to look. "You're in luck," I called back from the kitchen, having unearthed a bottle of red. Hannah sometimes used a splash of wine to marinate steaks, but this one remained unopened. I remedied that and poured a juice glass full, then handed it to Vince. "Sorry, I don't keep wine glasses," I told him.

He took a sip and grimaced.

"Christ, where'd you get this?"

"The grocery store, probably."

"This is furniture polish."

Even so he finished the glass.

"Would you like some more?" I asked.

"Of *this*? You want to give me more of *this* embalming fluid? Yeah, sure."

I refilled his glass, and apparently the refill didn't taste as much like Liquid Gold as the first, since he gulped it down without grimacing, and then held the glass out for another top-off.

"Is that why Marnie thinks I was snatched?" he asked as I poured. "Because Philly and my ex both got…damn."

"No. Philly reported your disappearance from a drug store."

"Oh, that. I wasn't taken, I just skipped out."

"Care to tell me why?"

"Believe me, Beauchamp, I didn't want to run out on Philly like that," he began. "But as soon as those letters started coming, he went on alert. He's got…had…this protection thing and he wouldn't leave my side. He actually asked if he could stay in our bedroom at night in case someone tried to break in. Now he's dead. Damn."

"You disappeared just to get away from him?"

"No, not to get away from him, at least not exclusively. I took off to get away from everything for a while. I needed some time to think without interference."

"Oh, right, that beach house you mentioned."

"No, not at the beach house, because if someone could find me at home or work they could find me there, too. After I slipped out of the drug store I found a place to rent a car and headed to Mission Hills and checked into a motel."

Mission Hills was a nondescript community that occupied the northern chunk of the San Fernando Valley which was probably best known for being close to other things.

"Why Mission Hills?" I asked.

"Who would think to look for someone in Mission Hills? The people who live there can't even find each other."

"Why do you think someone was looking for you?"

"Haven't you been paying attention? Those goddamn letters. They weren't asking for my autograph, you know. Then I got that text."

"What text?"

He reached into his pocket and pulled out his phone, and fingered through it until he pulled up a photo. He handed the phone over to me.

The picture on the screen was that of a dead fish lying on a doorstep.

"You know what that means?" he asked.

"It's a Mafia threat, isn't it?"

"Yeah. It's a warning that I'll be sleeping with the fishes."

"Death threats are now delivered via texting?"

"It's the modern era. Look, if I say I'm sorry for running out and making you think I was hijacked, can I have the rest of that slurry you've got there?"

I handed him the bottle. "If it's any consolation, I argued against Marnie's conviction that you were kidnapped, at least until the final letter which was a pre-ransom note."

"From who?"

"We don't know. And then there's this, which came in last night." I stepped to my phone machine and hit playback, letting the recorded voice fill the room: *"Dave, it's Vince Mazetta…They…they got Annemarie. Now they're coming for me…They know…they know…Aw, shit…they're here…"*

"What the hell is this?" Vince asked, looking flabbergasted. "That's not me! That doesn't even sound like me!"

"Actually, Vince, it does. Nobody thinks their recorded voice actually sounds like them."

"For Christ's sake, Beauchamp, I didn't make that call!"

An obvious fact hit me then…one so obvious I should have realized it when I first heard the message. "I believe you, Vince," I said. "I just now realized the voice on the phone said, 'Dave, it's Vince,' not 'Beauchamp, it's Vince.' I can't remember your ever calling me by my first name."

"Jesus," Vince said, shaking his head. "Somebody's pretending to be me. What the hell for?"

"To make me believe you've been abducted."

"That's screwy," he said, draining the bottle. "A fish-o-gram doesn't mean we're going to snatch you, it means we're going to kill you."

"Well, didn't both happen to Jimmy Hoffa?" I asked.

"Yeah, but..."

He fell silent for a moment then said, "I have a confession, Beauchamp."

"I think I already know," I replied. "You're not really in the outfit, are you?"

He leaned back. "I used to know a few of the guys socially, but no, I'm not really in the outfit."

"Why is the mob after you then?"

"You tell me. Maybe I turned one of their favorite ponies into Perfect Friends Special Export Canine Cuisine."

"Did Philly know this?"

"That I still use horsemeat?"

"That you're not really connected."

"I never had the heart to tell him it was just a performance. There are several of us who do it, businessmen mostly, and a few higher-ups in the movie racket. We're like re-enactors, Beauchamp, though instead of putting on Civil War uniforms and carrying swords, we wear Cyril Gore suits and pinkie rings. It would have crushed Philly to learn I'm a fraud. See, being my leg man made him feel important in a way he hadn't for a long time. His old man was one of Meyer Lansky's boys, so he grew up around the outfit. He's where I got a lot of my information about how to play the role. He'd talk about the old times when he was a driver for one of the retired dinosaurs in the last days of the Jewish mob. When the dinosaur died Philly had nothing, so I took him on and let him feel good about himself again. His being visible didn't really hurt my image, either."

"Do your kids think you're legit?"

"I never lied to any of my kids," Mazetta said forcefully. "Michael would sometimes get suspicious and ask me something, and I'd tell him I had no connection to the Mafia, that I was just a businessman, which is true. But he'd smile, because he assumed that was the lie. The other two never asked, frankly. It's not like we had thugs coming to the house on a regular basis. They all had pretty normal childhoods, except for...well, I won't speak ill of the dead. Despite everything, Annemarie didn't deserve to be murdered. Jesus, Beauchamp, what should I do now?"

"Go home and let Marnie know you're all right, for one thing" I said. "She's worried sick."

"One of the reasons I skipped after getting that text was because I didn't want to put her in harm's way. If I go back now, she's in danger too."

"Vince, what if something had happened to her while you were gone? How would you feel?"

"Like a louse in addition to being a fraud."

"Then go home."

The defeated man on my sofa was not the Vince Mazetta I knew, though I sensed it might be the real one. Now I understood his desire to present himself as a more powerful, even tacitly dangerous man.

Pay no attention to that man who's curtain has just fallen, the voice of Frank Morgan said inside my head.

"Okay, I'll go home," he said. "But I've still got another problem. It's the reason I came to see you in the first place. Somebody's following me."

"Who?"

"That's a fucking stupid question. How do I know who?"

The old Vince was beginning to return.

"Okay, what kind of car was the tail driving?"

"BMW, black, heavily-tinted windows."

"What about the plates?"

"No plate in front."

"How about the back?"

"Jesus, Beauchamp, I'm the one drinking but you're the one getting dopey! The car was tailing *me*, I wasn't tailing *it*. How could I see the rear plate? You got any more of this rotgut?"

I went and looked again but could not find another bottle. Then I pulled out a bottle of Tilex from under the sink and carried it back to him.

"Oh, you're a riot, Beauchamp," Vince said, trying very hard not to laugh.

At that moment my brain changed the subject and I realized that something in his story wasn't scanning. "You said you rented a car after you slipped out of the drug store, right?"

"Yeah, a Nissan something. Why?"

"How does the person tailing you know that car?"

"I don't get you."

"Let's assume your tail is the same person, or else is working with whoever has been sending you those letters. They would know the limo. They might even know your Mustang. But if you rented this car on the spur of the moment, how would they know what you're driving? They'd have to have seen you at the rental place. Unless…"

"You have a real bad habit of letting statements dangle, Beauchamp. Unless what?"

"Unless they're following the car and not you."

"Does that even make any sense?"

"Actually, it does. If they think whoever rented the car previously is still driving it, and that's really who they're tailing, then they're not tailing you. Stay here, I have an idea."

"What are you going to do?"

"Simply look outside for a black BMW with no plates and tinted windows. Don't go away."

I left the apartment and went out front, scanning the street on both sides.

A black Beemer had pulled up to the curb on the next block.

I began to stroll casually toward it, but halfway there—still too far for me to make out the plate—it suddenly pulled away and drove off.

It might have been a coincidence. It might have been a different black Beemer.

Or Vince might really be in trouble.

When I got back inside, I said to Vince, "The car was out there. It took off before I could see the plate."

"What should I do, Beauchamp," he said.

"Call a cab and go home," I suggested.

"Why a cab?"

"Because your shadow knows your rental car. Also because you've drained an entire bottle of wine and shouldn't drive."

"I had an entire bottle of something, anyway," he grumbled. "I'm not sure I'd dignify it with the term wine. Okay, I'll call an Uber. But what about my rental?"

"I'll return it tomorrow."

When he had finished calling for his ride, he shoved his phone back into his pocket and said, "I need to use your bathroom."

Upon his emergence the apartment suddenly filled with the sound of "Mambo Italiano"—it was Vince's ring tone. His Uber was on its way. I walked him down to the front door and asked for his car keys.

"All the paperwork's in the glove compartment," he said, handing the rental keys over. "The reservation was on my credit card…the one Marnie doesn't know I have…so you won't be able to sign for it. You'll have to pay cash."

"I still have the money you gave me for that car camera."

"Oh, right. Christ, that seems like such a long time ago."

He was right; it did.

When his ride pulled up he said, "You'll let me know what you learn about Philly, right? Annemarie, too?"

"I will. Be careful."

"Yeah."

I waited until he got into the Uber and pulled away. There was no sign of the BMW on the street.

I returned to my apartment just in time to catch the phone. This time it was Hannah.

"Hey, Dave, when were you thinking of coming back over here?" she asked.

"Well, I thought we'd agreed to dinner. Why, is something wrong?"

"No, no. Your mom went to the hospital and I guess I'm feeling a little lonely, is all.

"I'll tell you what. I have to return a rental car for Vince Mazetta, so how about I swing by the house, and you follow me over to the rental place in your car and then drive me back?"

"What if Ma Beauchamp comes back and I'm gone?"

"We'll leave a note for her telling her we'll be back soon."

"Okay."

"I'll be over as quickly as I can."

Unfortunately, in my zeal to make certain I didn't do something dumb like forget to ask for the car keys, I forgot to ask for the model and color of the Nissan something Vince had rented. So I stood on the sidewalk and pressed the door opener until a blue Altima at the curb flashed its lights.

So focused was I on getting used to the handling of the rental, and rather absently wondering what the attraction of either being around gangsters or pretending to be one yourself held for some people, that I paid little attention to the car passing me on Ventura Boulevard. I mean, this is L.A.... who pays attention to other cars?

Maybe that's why the driver felt he had to shatter my side window with a bullet, which screamed past my head so closely it brushed my hair.

He was trying to get my attention.

THIRTEEN

Fighting panic, I pulled the car over to the curb where I got out careful-ly and shook the glass shards off of me. I felt a warm trickle running down my neck and a sharp pain under my right ear; a tiny speck of safety glass was embedded there. I managed to get it out without cutting my fingers.

Since the passenger window was intact, the bullet had not passed straight through and out the other side.

After a quick search, I found a dent in the metal door handle on the pas-senger side, and through further examination located the slug on the floor. It must have bounced off.

After carefully picking it up, I slipped it into my shirt pocket and then speed-dialed Dane Colfax.

He must have recognized my number on his caller ID because he an-swered, "For God's sake, Beauchamp, I'm just about to leave! Who's dead now?"

"Almost me. Somebody took a shot at me while I was driving."

"Have you ever thought of taking up a new career as a skeet?"

"Thanks for your concern."

"Are you dead?"

"Obviously not."

"Injured?"

"Small glass cut on my neck."

"Then you're welcome. I don't suppose you got a look at who did it."

"I saw a car come around me but I didn't pay attention to it. After the shot, I was a little distracted."

"Didn't somebody take a pop at you once before?"

"That was at my office. This was just a couple blocks from my apart-ment."

"You might want to think about moving."

"They weren't trying to kill me, Dane, they were trying to kill Vince Mazetta."

"You were just practice?"

"I was driving his rental car."

"When was this?"

"Just a short time ago."

"So he's no longer vanished?"

"No. He was here and he's fine, though he said somebody was following him. I caught sight of a black BMW in front of my building, but it took off before I could read a plate. I suspect the driver doubled back around, saw the rental on the street, then pulled around and took a shot at me, not realizing it wasn't Vince behind the wheel. But I can't prove anything."

"You call the locals yet?"

"No, and I'm not going to this time. I'd like you to write up the report on this one."

"Didn't I mention I'm not even supposed to be working today?"

"Yes, but I'd appreciate it. When I return the car, the folks at…"

I glanced down at the key ring in my hand…

"…Travis Rental Car, they're going to ask for a police report to go along with the shattered window, and I don't want to wait an hour or so for North Hollywood's finest to show up and take notes."

"They should be used to it by now."

"Those were Van Nuys' finest. My office is in a different precinct."

"We don't have precincts, we have divisions."

"Fine, whatever. I still want to give the information to you then I won't call you again for the rest of the day."

"If you do, I won't answer. Okay, give me the damn information."

I rattled off everything I knew about what had happened, and after which added, "You know, maybe you should keep Vince Mazetta's name off the report. Just say I was returning a rental car."

"Anything else you want me to conceal?"

"No, and thanks. I owe you one."

"You owe me a dozen."

"You're probably right. Bye, Dane."

I cut off the call and climbed back into the driver's seat, putting my butt down on it very gingerly just in case I'd missed some of the glass.

Since driving on a freeway next to a shattered window wasn't the best of ideas, I took surface streets to my folks' house, and arrived there in fairly good time. When I rang the bell, Hannah answered.

"Dave, you're bleeding!" she cried.

"Only a little," I said, walking in. "Is Mom still at the hospital?"

"Yes." She examined my neck and face. "What happened?"

"Somebody shot at me."

"Shot at you? That's it. You're getting out of this business!"

"Yeah, yeah, I know," I acknowledged out loud for the first time. "But I still have to finish this case."

"What if it finishes you first?"

I had no answer.

"Come on," she said, taking my arm. "There must be some peroxide and gauze in the bathroom."

We couldn't find any in the downstairs bath so we tried upstairs. After hunting through nearly every cabinet, Hannah finally turned up a bottle of witch hazel and some bandages, and began cleaning the stream of dried blood.

"It's not bad," she said, "though another half-inch over and it might have hit the carotid artery. This looks like a puncture, not a bullet graze."

"It's from a piece of flying safety glass," I told her.

"Right. Safety."

"I think it slowed the bullet down enough that it didn't go through the other window. Or me."

She shook her head as she carefully patched me up, sealing it with a kiss. Then she put the bandages and witch hazel back in the cabinet under the sink, but stopped before closing the door. "What's this?" Hannah asked, picking up a medical bottle. "This shouldn't be down here—it should be with all the others in the medicine chest." After reading the label, her eyes grew wide.

"What is it?" I asked.

"Prescription medicine for your dad," she replied. "Viagra."

"*Viagra*? Let me see that."

It was in Dad's name all right, and a thirty-day supply, though I had no idea whether the doctor's name on the label was his regular guy or a specialist. "Why would he need Viagra?" I asked.

"Why does anyone need Viagra?" Hannah replied. "They aren't like you."

"Why hide it down here, though?"

"Well…maybe he doesn't want Ma Beauchamp to know he needs a little assistance."

"Or he doesn't want her to know…oh, man."

The prescription was for thirty pills and was dated to the beginning of the month. I took a Kleenex and laid it down on the counter, then poured out the pills and counted them. Six of them were gone. "You use this stuff on an as-needed basis, right?" I asked Hannah.

"I'm not really an expert, but I think so. One of the senior adjustors at you-know-where used to do personal analyses of new young female recruits, if you know what I mean. He relied on this stuff."

I carefully put the pills back into the container.

Then something struck me. "Could taking this have led to Dad's heart attack?"

"Wow, that's a good question," Hannah said. "I've heard that Viagra is beneficial to the heart and circulation for some people but for others… yeah, it's possible this could have made him sick, particularly if he already had an undiagnosed heart condition. Maybe we should tell his doctor at the hospital."

"I'll take care of that," I said, sticking the pill bottle back under the sink. "But there's something I'd like you to do, and it won't be easy. Talk to Mom and find out if…well, I mean, if she…"

"Dave, if Carl's taking Viagra, she must have noticed something unusual, unless he's…oh!" She actually put her hand over her mouth as she caught on to my suspicion that Mom was not the beneficiary of the pills. "Do you really think your Dad is cheating on her?"

I raised my arms and shrugged. In truth I had a pretty good suspicion he was, given that Mom admitted to being on the cusp of seventy; I simply didn't want to say it out loud.

"Let's try to find out if these pills might have bearing on his condition," I said. "We'll worry about why he's taking them later. Right now I have to turn the rental car in, shot-out window or not."

After finding the closest Travis office the old-fashioned way—looking in the Yellow Pages Mom had by the phone—I headed out to Culver City, with Hannah following me in her Mini Cooper. I prepared my spiel on the way and delivered it fairly convincingly to the clerk, who inspected the car and opted to agree with my story that some unknown projectile had been propelled up by the wheels of another car and hit the window, then bounced off.

He didn't notice the dent in the door handle.

I told them the man who had rented the car was so shaken that he was home resting, which is why I was returning it.

And since I had changed my story to omit the fact that I was shot at, I did not mention that I'd filed a police report.

I hoped Dane wouldn't mind.

"Fortunately Mr. Mazetta took out insurance when he rented the vehicle," the young, Nordic-looking clerk said. "So it's covered."

"Yes, Mr. Mazetta is a careful man," I offered. "I'm curious, though. Do you see this sort of thing a lot?"

"Not a lot, but we've seen it, though normally it's the windshield that gets hit and shattered from something that's shot up from the tires of a vehicle in front, usually a truck. That's much more dangerous for the driver. You were actually pretty lucky."

"Yeah, my guardian angel was watching out for me."

When the paperwork was all finished and I'd paid out of Vince's money, Hannah and I drove back.

Mom was there waiting for us. She looked fatigued, but not distraught.

"They're now talking about putting in a stent," she said. "Honestly, I've heard so many variations of his condition and what they're planning on doing about it, I'm not sure I know what's happening."

"As long as he's stable, it will be all right," Hannah said.

"He was asking for you, Dave," Mom went on. "He said there's something he needs to tell you."

"I'd like to talk to him, too," I said. "Maybe I should go there now."

"He was sleeping when I left. Give him a little time. Good lord, what did you do to yourself?"

I fingered the bandage on my neck. "Oh, I, uh, got a new razor."

Mom shook her head. "Sometimes I think I'm the only one in this family who isn't trying to commit suicide. To prove that, I'm going to lie down for a bit."

After she'd gone Hannah said, "This is really hard on her."

"I'm sure it is."

"You don't look all that great either."

"I found a body in my office."

"What?"

"Vince Mazetta's right-hand man, a guy named Philly, was killed in my office."

"Dave, what's happening?"

"Too much all at once."

"I don't want to be constantly worried about you getting shot at or finding cadavers in your office," she said. "You have to make a choice, Dave. Be a detective or be with me."

"That's no choice," I said. "You win hands down. I just have to—"

"Finish this case. Yeah, I know. Is it really that important?"

"It is. Then I promise I won't even renew my license. Maybe I'll rent a movie theatre somewhere and start a classic Hollywood film festival."

"Would that make you happy?"

"Yeah. I think it would."

"Okay. I guess I'd better start preparing for dinner."

"We're not going out?"

"I don't think Ma Beauchamp's up for it. I peeked in the freezer earlier and found a package of frozen pork loin, so I was thinking of making schnitzel. That's pounded pork, breaded and pan fried. It's really good."

"It sounds good."

"Your mom eats fried stuff, right?"

"As far as I know."

While she was being Hannah Homemaker, I went back into the living room. My cell rang a minute or so later. It was Marnie, thanking me for convincing Vince to go home.

"Detective Colfax called and wanted to talk to Vince," she went on. "Then he asked questions that implied Vince was a suspect."

"That's their job, it's routine," I said.

Marnie also mentioned that one-by-one Vince's kids had called (having been notified by the police) and that they were working on setting up a conference call between everybody later that night.

"Any more letters?" I asked.

"No, none today. But if Vince simply dropped out for a few days, what was all that business of 'We have him' in the last letter?"

"I don't know yet, Marnie, though I'm quickly coming to the conclusion that the letters are designed to scare him rather than deliver an actual threat. To be honest, I think we're dealing with an amateur, someone who is acting out what he's seen on TV. I do intend to find out, though."

"Thanks, Dave. And even if he doesn't say it, Vince thanks you, too. Oh, you did get that rental car back safely, right?"

"I got it back, yes."

After a few more pleasantries, we signed off.

I had no sooner settled into the living room sofa and turned on the television when the house phone rang. We let it go through to the machine, but when I heard, "Hello, Mrs. Beauchamp, I'm calling from the nursing station at Cedars…" I leaped for it.

"Hello, this is Dave Beauchamp, Carl's son," I said. "What's happening?"

"Oh, Mr. Beauchamp, good," the nurse said. "You're the one we were hoping to reach."

"Is Dad all right?"

"Yes, he is. He's awake and has been asking for you. He says there is something vitally important he has to tell you."

"Do you know what it is?"

"I'm simply passing along the message. He is fine to receive visitors."

"I'll be there as soon as I can," I said.

Turning to Hannah I explained the call and asked to borrow her Mini Cooper, then told her I'd be back for dinner.

At least I hoped I would be.

Parking at Cedars was challenging, but finding Dad in the hospital took only slightly less effort than tracking a teenage runaway. I finally located him in a regular ward, having been transferred out of the ICU. He looked weak, but more or less like himself. When I walked into the room he smiled.

"Hey, Davy. Thanks for coming. This might be the last time we actually speak."

"Come on, Dad, I didn't come here to give you last rights."

"They're going to cut open my chest and play around with my exposed heart."

"And they're trained professionals who have done it before for lots of people who went on to live for decades more."

"All right. But humor me, okay? If something were to go wrong, you need to know where my will and all of my papers are. That's not depression, it's simply planning. I haven't told you yet, but you're going to be the executor of my will."

"Okay."

"There's a small safe in the corner of the clothes closet in my bedroom. Do you have something to write with?"

I had my pad on me but had to go to the nurse's station to borrow a pen. I returned to the room ready. Dad reeled off the combination numbers to the safe and I carefully wrote them down.

"There's some cash in there, too, which goes to your mother," he said.

"Speaking of Mom, shouldn't she be here to witness all this?"

"Oh, Pammy doesn't know from legal matters. You do. Besides, there's something I need to tell you about your mom and me."

Taking a deep breath I said, "Dad, I think I know."

"You do? How'd you find out?"

"Hannah was looking in the cabinet in your bathroom for a bandage because I cut myself, and she found the pill bottle."

"You found my stash of Viagra?"

"Yes. We weren't looking for it."

He chuckled. "And since your mom would be in a lot better mood if she was getting the big one, you're worried that I'm cheating on her with someone else, right?"

"What really worries both Hannah and me is that your taking Viagra might have caused your attacks."

He leaned up to study my face, then his head fell back to the pillow. "Oh for Christ's sake, I never even considered that. Boy, there really is no fool like an old fool, is there?"

Since there was no good response to that, I said nothing.

"Trust me, Davy, I'm not cheating on your mother. Not legally, anyway."

"What does that mean?"

"It means I'm in a physical relationship with a paralegal at the office who looks like Maureen O'Hara on her best day. That's what the pills were for, though if they're going to kill me, to hell with them."

"Is this some kind of lawyerese?" I asked. "You're sleeping with a paralegal who's, what, my age? Younger? And it's not cheating?"

"She's not your age or younger. She's forty-seven and has a few wrinkles, a couple of stretch marks, red hair, and a body that won't stop. She's a divorcee and we have no illusions. We get together, we have sex, and we like it. She can do things I've never experienced before. When we're finished, we say goodbye and plan to meet up again later. No roses next morning, no phone calls, none of that Doris Day-Rock Hudson stuff. We're two people with physical needs who have figured out how to satisfy them with no collateral damage. Occasionally we go to lunch together, but we don't have sex on the table in the restaurant."

"Dad, pretend I'm the world's biggest idiot and explain to me how this is not cheating on your wife."

"I'm not cheating on your mother because she is not my wife."

I wasn't sure I'd heard right. "Mom…is…not…"

"We've been divorced for twelve years now."

Ladies and gentlemen, this is Orson Welles…The next sound you hear will be that of Dave Beauchamp's head exploding.

FOURTEEN

"I guess this is a bit of a shock, huh?" Dad said.

"No, Dad," I replied. "Learning that John Wayne was gay and Chill Wills was his lover would be a *bit* of a shock. This is magnitude eight. How can you be divorced?"

"The usual way. We each got lawyers…actually, I got them for both of us…and then a judge decreed we were divorced. It was completely amicable, Davy."

"But you still live together."

"Yeah, that. Well, see…is there any way to raise this bed up?"

I monkeyed around with an attached control box until the head of the bed started to automatically lift.

"Thanks," he said. "It was like this. When you left for college, you took a lot of energy with you. That house seemed awfully damned empty."

So it's my fault? Bette Davis barked inside my head, but I didn't pass it on. I just listened.

"After a while it became increasingly clear that the only thing your mom and I had in common anymore was you. I know we each treated you a little differently. Your mom wanted you to be perfect, which, of course, no one can be. I was more willing to let you be you. Well, once you were gone, she turned on me and expected me to be perfect, but that train had pulled out of the station long ago. I'm not a perfect person. Nobody is. Anyway, she started retreating into books and I spent most of my home time watching movies or golfing on the weekends and, after a while, we were the proverbial ships that passed in the night. That's all we did in the night, too, since a combination of her age and 'the Change' had a cooling effect on her. Sorry if that's too much information. Funny thing is I still have dreams about sleeping with your mother every now and then. Of all the women my subconscious could fantasize about at night, it's still her. I guess we're at that stage where 'In your dreams, pal,' is the literal truth."

Since I was unable to think of any intelligent response, I said nothing.

"Anyway, we attempted to carry on like nothing was wrong, while the elephant in the room just kept eating more and getting bigger. Finally, about your sophomore year of college, we decided the marriage was going nowhere and it was time to cut our losses. Neither of us wanted to hurt the other, which is unusual in divorces, and we worked out a deal pretty quickly. We went through the motions, and got a divorce on the grounds of irreconcilable differences. I found a place and moved out, and Pam kept the house, which was part of the deal. We'd speak on the phone every so often, and even went out to dinner a time or two. Then something strange happened. Is there any water in here?"

I found a plastic water pitcher and poured a glass for him. When he was finished drinking, he smiled and said, "You know, this is probably the longest I've ever actually spoken to you about something other than old movies."

"I think you're right," I acknowledged. "But don't stop now. What was the strange thing that happened?"

"I concluded I didn't like living alone. It was a form of solitary confinement. If you're living with another person, even if you don't talk to them, you still know they're there, and that's a comforting feeling. So it was... hell, I guess it was right after we attended your commencement together... I went to Pam and asked if I might be able to move back in. Still stay divorced, and all, but move back in and share the house again. I'd live there and pay for everything like I used to instead of sending an alimony check each month. I didn't know what to expect from her, but once she ascertained I was serious, she grinned a little and said, 'I wish you would. The upstairs toilet tank is leaking, the back door sticks, and the goldfish won't do anything I tell it.' So I moved back and stayed back. Since your old room was vacant, I took it. To be honest, after all those years of proclaiming how she was 'the only one in the house' who did this, that, or the other thing, I think she was getting awfully tired of being the only one in the house, period."

"And you never thought of remarrying?" I asked.

"Oh, idly. But things were working. We didn't get in each other's hair as much because the pressure was off. We were friends, not spouses. I put a DVD player in your bedroom so I can watch whatever old movies I want. Pam goes to her book club every month, and she even started volunteering at the library. We usually take meals together, but not always. We both have a sense of support from the other, but also a sense of freedom. Then there's the Viagra thing. Your mom felt bad about no longer wanting to... you know. In her mind it was a form of failure, and you know how much she hates failure. So now it's not an issue because we're divorced. And it's just physical, Davy. Colleen is not going to become your new mom."

"Colleen?"

"Maureen O'Hara."

"Ah. Does she know about your situation?"

"She knows I'm divorced, just like she is. She knows I'm not thinking of marriage or anything like that, and neither is she. Good lord, Davy, you remember college, don't you? Your hormones are raging so you sleep with as many girls as you can, knowing you're not tying yourself down for a lifetime. It's purely physical, right?"

The idea that my father in his sixties was getting more action than I had in college was almost as depressing as getting shot at.

"Did you or Mom ever plan to tell me this before your attack?" I asked.

"Well, neither of us particularly wanted the judgment."

"Judgment?"

"You can be a little judgmental at times."

Young Dr. Metcalf chose that moment to come into the room to check on Dad.

"He's doing as well as can be expected," the doctor said. "We're scheduling the procedure for Monday."

"Do I need to be here?" I asked.

"I'm assuming your mother will be, so if you want to keep her company in the waiting room it might help her."

"Okay. I guess I'll take off now, Dad, unless there's something else."

"You've got the combination, right?"

I tapped my shirt pocket where I'd stuck the note, and also felt the bullet which was still living there.

"Now what, Davy?" Dad said.

"Now what what?"

"You just did that thing with your face again, like you had a sudden terrible thought."

"It's nothing, Dad. Really."

"If you say so. I just hope you never get in a high-stakes poker game, because you'll end up losing everything but your nuts."

See? Even your father knows "you're nuts," Robert Mitchum said in my head.

"You did it again, just now," Dad said.

"I guess I reacted to the thought of losing my nuts," I replied.

"If you need a good urologist I can recommend one," Dr. Metcalf said helpfully.

I left Dad and Doogie Houser and headed back down to the lobby, where a very striking looking redhead was asking the receptionist direction's to Dad's room. She was holding a vase of flowers with an attached balloon that set *Get Well Soon*, and did indeed look like Maureen O'Hara, circa *McLintock!* Sure, I could have walked up and introduced myself, but I opted not to.

Given the flowers and her concerned expression, though, I wondered if she was taking their relationship a little more seriously than Dad's characterization of it as a hook-up.

When I got home, Mom was up and helping Hannah in the kitchen.

"What was it your father wanted to tell you?" she said by way of *hello*.

"He told me where to find certain paperwork, just in case," I replied, giving Hannah a peck on the back of the neck.

"Just in case of what?"

"He's worried, Mom. He's afraid something's going to go wrong in the surgery, which is scheduled for Monday, by the way."

"That man is going to worry himself into the grave even without the surgery. His doctors seemed pretty optimistic."

"They still are. They just have to convince Dad to stop being a lawyer long enough to get well."

"What do you mean stop being a lawyer?"

"A good trial lawyer never asks a question he doesn't already know the answer to," I said, repeating an adage I'd heard about a thousand times in the classroom. "Dad's a good trial lawyer, but day after tomorrow he's going to be wheeled into a room where he doesn't have all the answers, and it's making him jittery."

"He told you that?"

"No, but it's pretty easy to see. It's also pretty easy to see he's not going to be able to go back to work any time soon, if at all. First thing Monday, before his procedure, I'll swing by the firm and return the files so Len Allen can reassign the cases. "

Mom didn't respond. Instead she pulled a bag of egg noodles from the pantry and set it on the counter. Then she took me by the elbow and started to maneuver me out of the kitchen, calling back to Hannah, "I'll be right back, dear."

"What's up, Mom?" I asked, but she remained silent until she had led me to the corner of the living room that was furthest from the kitchen.

"Dave, you might be asked to sign some official papers on Monday," she said in hushed tones. "Papers that I...can't sign. Oh, god, I don't want to tell you this, but it looks like I have to."

"It's all right, Mom, Dad told me."

"He did? About the..."

Divorce, I silently mouthed.

"You must think we're a couple of old fools."

"Look, I won't lie and tell you I wasn't floored, but if that's what works for you, then who am I to judge?"

"In spite of everything, I don't want to lose him."

"I know. Did you tell Hannah?"

Mom shook her head.

"Then let's keep it in the family for the time being," I suggested.

Hannah's schnitzel and noodle dinner proved to be excellent, so much so that Mom actually asked how she made it.

After the dishes were taken care of, I said we needed to go. Hannah offered to stay over, but Mom said she would be fine.

It was nearly eight o'clock when we got back to the apartment. During the ride I had convinced Hannah to trade up to a larger car once we had the money…or at least buy a larger car in addition to keeping the Mini, since it had been Palmer Hanley's and she felt sentimental about it.

A quick check of the phone machine showed no messages, for which I was grateful.

I seriously needed time to sit and think.

About everything.

"Are you all right, Dave?" Hannah asked, petting my arm.

"It's been kind of a stressful day," I said.

Getting shot at will do that to a person, Edward G. Robinson said inside my head.

"I think I'm going to draw a tub full of water and just sit in it for a while," I added.

"Do you want me to scrub your back?"

"I just need to veg out for a little bit, okay?"

"I'm here if you need me."

I smiled and kissed her nose, which always makes her wrinkle it up, like Elizabeth Montgomery in *Bewitched*. It's a Pavlovian reaction that's so cute it would make me queasy coming from anyone else.

I carried a notepad and pen into the bathroom with me and sat on the toilet while the water was running in the tub. There was nothing I could do about Dad's situation except take those files back to his office. The rest was in his doctor's hands.

On Monday morning, literally.

I expected the truce with Mom to hold as well, though I still felt pretty schmucky for snapping at her the way I did in the hospital.

Instead I concentrated on the Mazetta case.

On the notepad I began a second draft of my list of case points, hoping that writing it all down might somehow establish clarity, or a pattern, or *something*. At the top I jotted: *1) Vince gets threatening letters*.

Then:

2) Vince suspects "goombahs."

3) Vince seems to vanish; wife Marnie thinks he's been kidnapped.

4) Vince's ex-wife Annemarie is murdered by strangulation.

5) Philly Lepkowitz is murdered by a gunshot.

6) Vince returns; he was really hiding after receiving the Mafia "fish" photo

I made a *6A)* to note that Vince's mob-boss act was literally that, but good enough that some real mobsters might believe it.

Then:

6B) How many real mobsters are there in L.A.? After thinking another moment, I added: *Are they all play-acting?*

The tub was full enough now so I stripped down and settled in, keeping my pad and pen within arm's reach. The warm, lapping water reminded me of when I was a kid and used to take baths all the time instead of showers. My dad once told me that transitioning to the shower was a sign of impending adulthood, along with preferring mustard to ketchup on a hotdog, showing more interest in girls than comic books, and realizing that Jimmy Stewart was a better actor than Spencer Tracy.

After soaking for about ten minutes I heard Hannah call through the door, "Everything all right?"

"Fine," I called back.

"Don't get all shriveledy."

After another ten minutes the water was seriously cooling. I could either run more hot in the tub and stay a bit longer, or simply get out. Since I was starting to get a little shriveledy, I opted for the latter.

I called through the door, "Hannah, do we have a clean towel?"

"Let me check," she called back. Then, a minute later, she stepped into the bathroom with a towel wrapped around her naked body like a sarong, saying, "Oops," as she dropped it onto the floor. Never taking her eyes off of me, she bent over to pick it up, then stepped into the tub and began to dry me.

It was only partially successful; we were still damp when we got to the bedroom.

Soon, so were the sheets.

FIFTEEN

Sunday arrived along with the morning paper.

Hannah was the first up so she went down to the lobby to get it. There were only a handful of us in the building that took the Sunday *Times*, but you still had to be quick to make sure someone didn't snatch a copy from the stack dropped at the lobby door.

I managed to stay in bed for another hour or so. I had nothing on the agenda today except checking in with Dad at the hospital, and then synchronize with Mom when to be there tomorrow for his surgery.

I hoped it stayed that way.

Fat chance, William Conrad's voice rumbled inside my head. You remember him; *Cannon* on television and, decades before that, a B-movie heavy in all senses of the word.

A little before noon a woman from Travis Rental Car called wanting to speak with Vince. "We haven't been able to reach him at the number he gave us," she said.

I promised I would have him contact them as soon as I could.

After hanging up with her, I figured it was time to check in with Dad. He was in better spirits today and after a minute I found out why: Colleen was there.

"I saw her yesterday," I told him. "You're right. She does look like Maureen O'Hara."

"You saw her? Where?"

"In the lobby. Don't worry, I didn't say anything. But if you don't mind, I'd like to speak with her now. Could you hand over the phone?"

"Well, I don't know…"

"I'm not going to say anything rude, Dad. I just want to talk to her."

After a pause, a woman's voice said, "Hello."

"Hi, this is Carl's son Dave. I just wanted to introduce myself and say that I know about the situation with you two, and I'm not going to make trouble. In fact if you'd give me your number, I can call you and let you know when my mom and I will be there tomorrow, so there are no accidental meetings."

"I wasn't really planning on being here tomorrow," Colleen said. "I have to go into work. But if you would keep me informed on how things went, I'd appreciate it."

She gave me a number indicating the west side and then said, "I'm glad we talked. Here's your father."

"Hey, Davy," he said. "Everything copacetic?

"Yep. Mom and I will be by tomorrow before you go into surgery. Is there anything you want me to bring?"

"A new heart."

After I hung up, Hannah came in and said, "You know, I really wish you wouldn't leave that bullet lying around. It makes me uncomfortable."

It was the slug I retrieved from the rental car. I had taken it out of my pocket and laid it down on the kitchen counter without thinking.

"Oh, sorry. I need to get it to the police anyway."

I stuck it in my pants pocket, along with the undecipherable note I found in my office building and the scrap of paper with Colleen's number.

For the first time I realized I had never asked for her last name, in order to call her at the firm.

Well, there can't be that many attractive middle-aged women named Colleen sleeping with my dad.

After cursorily perusing the paper, I decided I'd wasted enough time. I got out my phone to call Vince and break the news that the car place wanted to talk to him.

Marnie answered.

"Vince is a little distracted right now," she said. "He's been having to deal with the police about both Annemarie and Philly, plus talking to his kids. It's rather upset his normal routine.

Yes, murder can do that to you, William Powell wisecracked inside my head.

In the background I heard Vince say, "Now who's calling?"

"It's Dave Beauchamp," Marnie told him, and a few seconds later Vince got on the phone.

"The cops want to know where I was when Philly was killed," he said. "Can you believe that?"

"Actually I can," I told him. "I presume you have an alibi."

"Sure I have an alibi. People from both that motel in Mission Hills and the barbecue joint down the street saw me."

"But Mission Hills isn't all that far from my office in Sherman Oaks," I said. "You could have left the motel with no one seeing you, driven down to pop Philly, and then gone back."

"Who the hell's side are you on, Beauchamp?" he cried. "Is that why you called, just to harass me?"

"No, I'm calling to let you know that Travis Rental Car contacted me and said they need to talk with you. Oh, jeez…since I haven't spoken to you since I returned your car, I didn't get the chance to tell you someone took a shot at me while I was driving."

"Someone *what*?"

I gave him the rundown, after which I heard him mutter, "I don't believe it."

"I think whoever it was thought I was you."

"Well, that's comforting. You call the police?"

"Yes, my friend Colfax. I asked him to make out the report, but I didn't tell Travis that it was a gunshot. I just said something hit the car window, like a stone."

"I'll tell you what. We'll go down to the rental joint together. In fact, now that Philly's gone, you can be my driver."

"I'll go with you to the car place but I'm not looking for a job as a driver. I'll be there within the hour."

I was more worried about breaking the news to Hannah that I had to leave again, but she took it well.

"I'm letting you do whatever you need to do because I know this is your last case," she said. "*Right*?"

"Right."

On the way to Vince's place I had to pull into the gas station and buy lunch for my Corolla, and instinctively looked around for a black BMW while I was pumping. Finding none, I fought the traffic the rest of the way to Casa Mazetta.

It seemed strange to pull through the gate without seeing Philly hanging around. Marnie met me at the door and ushered me inside. Vince was on the sofa, dressed more casually than usual in a golf shirt and light green slacks. With him was another young man whose resemblance to Vince identified him as one of his sons. It turned out to be his middle kid, Paul, the assistant director.

"You're the PI?" Paul asked me after rising to shake my hand. He was several inches taller than his father, which wasn't saying much. "Bad casting."

"We can't all be Stacy Keach," I said, adding, "I'm sorry for your loss."

"Thanks."

"Vickie's coming down as soon as she can," Marnie said. "Have you heard anything more about Philly?"

I shook my head. "Did he have any family? The police will probably want to know."

"His parents are long gone," Vince said, "and he had a brother who went down in a bad drug bust sometime in the eighties. I know of only one other relative, his nephew, but he was killed in combat in Afghanistan about ten years ago. If there is someone else out there Philly never mentioned them."

After more small talk and reiteration that I was not making much progress on any front, I borrowed Vince to go to the Travis office.

"Here," he said, tossing me the keys to the limo which was parked in the garage. "You ever drive a limo?"

"No."

"Aw, you'll love it!"

From my perspective the car looked like the Queen Mary. "Good god, are you sure you want me to drive this?"

"I have a hard time reaching the pedals, all right?" Vince snapped.

"Sorry," I said, getting behind the wheel.

"Not half as sorry as I am. To you I'm five-two. To Marnie I'm four-eleven-and-a-half, because I take off my shoes. In the mirror, though, I'm six-one, like Dean Martin."

"Dino wore lifts, too," I told him. "He was really only five-ten."

"Shut up and drive."

Handling the Caddy proved not quite as daunting as I'd feared, though I still drove carefully.

"You know, Vince, we should probably go over our stories before getting to the rental place," I called over my shoulder.

"What are you talking about? You're the one who was fired upon."

"Right, but I sort of intimated you were in the car at the time."

"Oh, great, thanks."

"And you did tell me you were being followed, though I think we should maybe not mention that."

"Tell me what to say, then."

I went through the story…at least my version of the story…including the truth about the car, driver, or any passenger, which was that the sudden shock of the window shattering blocked out anything I might have observed.

"And you don't know why they have to verify all this with me?" Vince asked.

"Honestly, I don't know what they want, though it's probably nothing more than some insurance paperwork that needs to be filled out. They said they tried calling the number you left but never got through."

"Yeah, that makes sense," he acknowledged. "It rang a few times but I didn't recognize the number so I ignored it. The only person I spoke with the whole time I was gone was Philly."

Even though we weren't at a corner, I slammed on the brakes, and nearly propelled Vince into the front seat, since he wasn't wearing a seatbelt.

"What the fuck, Beauchamp?" he cried.

There was a car behind me who pulled around and passed, but nobody shot at me this time.

"When did you talk to Philly?" I demanded.

"The night before I came back. Friday, I guess. Why? What's with the third degree?"

"What did you talk about, Vince?"

"Would you mind driving the car? If someone's tailing us, stopping in the street like this makes us sitting ducks!"

I gave gas to the limo and repeated, "What did you talk about?"

"I got sick of him calling my cell every half hour so I finally answered. That's all. The big goombah actually started crying when he heard my voice."

"This is important, Vince…did you tell him where you were?"

"The motel? Yeah, I told him. Why is that important?"

I pulled the Caddy to a stop, but this time for a light. I used the opportunity to look back at him. "Because somebody followed you from Mission Hills, even though you were driving an unfamiliar car. That means they knew where you were staying. If you told Philly where you were, he must have told the person who followed you."

"Why would he do that? Philly wouldn't rat anyone out unless you had a gun pointed at him. Oh…oh, shit…"

I could tell Vince finally got it.

I had no proof, of course, but you didn't have to be Philip Marlowe to figure that Philly told someone about Vince, either innocently or with a gun pointed at his heart, and that person subsequently drove to the motel in Mission Hills and then waited for Vince to leave then followed him back to my apartment.

Where he tried to shoot him and got me instead.

There you go again, Slick, the voice of Lauren Bacall said inside my head. *Leaving out the women.*

Right.

Where he *or she* tried to kill me.

By the time I reached the rental car place in Culver City, I'd half-convinced myself to go out and buy a Cadillac limo or a town car for Hannah, to replace the Mini Cooper.

Or maybe we'd keep the Mini in the trunk for emergencies.

"This isn't where I got the car," Vince said.

"I know, but it's where I returned it," I told him. "They're all connected by computer."

The Travis Rental Car clerk—the same Nordic guy I'd spoken to earlier—must have seen us pull in to the lot because once we were inside, he said, "I know you're not returning *that*."

"No, but I'm Dave Beauchamp, remember? You wanted to get in touch with Mr. Mazetta, who rented the car with the broken window."

"Oh, right. It's actually our manager who wants to talk to you. She's with another customer right now, so hold on a minute."

We sat in the molded-plastic chairs and watched as a handful of people came in either to rent or return vehicles.

None of them reported gunfire.

Finally a stylish-looking, dark-haired woman wearing a blue company blazer over a gray skirt came toward us. "Mr. Mazetta?" she asked, and Vince stood up. "I'm Bobbie Quinlan, nice to meet you." Then turning to me she said, "You're the fellow who returned the car, right?"

"Yes, I'm Dave Beauchamp."

"Fine, fine, please come this way, gentlemen."

We were ushered behind the counter and into a private office that was functional in a no-frills kind of way, and asked to sit down again. Bobbie Quinlan took a seat behind the desk and picked up a small stack of papers.

"Is anything wrong?" I asked.

"Wrong? No, no, nothing wrong. Just paperwork, you know. Our insurance company wants every 'I' crossed and 'T' dotted!"

She smiled at her own joke.

"I see you only drove the car fifty-seven miles."

"That sounds right," Vince said. "Why, is there a minimum or something?"

"No, no. It's just that most renters go longer distances. Out of state, often."

"Well, I just needed some wheels for in-town, because…"

"Because your car was in the shop," I offered.

"Right," Vince said.

"Fine, fine," Bobbie Quinlan said. "Basically what the insurance company is asking for is whether you have car insurance of your own."

"Isn't that mandatory?" I asked.

"You'd be surprised how many people maneuver around that."

"Of course I'm insured," Vince said, "but the guy at the other office sold me on the idea of being completely safe."

The manager didn't see his quick ironic glance in my direction.

"Of course, of course. Might I get your information, though?"

Vince pulled out his wallet and produced his insurance card. As he did so, a photo fell out onto the floor. I picked it up and saw three people, one of whom was Paul Mazetta. I assumed the slightly older man and the young girl standing with him were Vince's other children, Michael and Vickie.

Vickie was what is no longer acceptable to say out loud: a real looker. She was a honey blonde with large eyes, a delicate nose, and a perfect smile.

After receiving the insurance card, Ms. Quinlan excused herself and went off to make a photocopy of it.

"I hope she won't need my birth certificate too," Vince grumbled.

"You dropped this," I said, handing the photo to him.

"Oh, thanks. These are the kids."

"I figured that."

He smiled before sticking it back in his wallet.

Bobbie Quinlan returned a minute later and gave the card back, then slid over a document authorizing the company to contact Vince's insurance agent if necessary. "Merely a formality," she said.

Even so, both Vince and I read the document carefully. He glanced at me and I nodded. Then he took the proffered pen and signed.

"Thank you," the woman said, scooping up the papers and rising.

"That it?" Vince asked.

"Yes, that's all. I'm sorry for the inconvenience, but we can't accept an electronic signature. You know what they say…the more things stay the same, the more they change."

She chuckled at that one too as she escorted us out of her office.

The rental area was now completely empty.

"Not a lot of business today," Vince commented.

"It comes and goes," Bobbie Quinlan replied. "Location has a lot to do with it. We get nowhere near the business of say, the offices at LAX, or even SNA."

I stopped cold. "I'm sorry, what did you say? LAX and what?"

"SNA. It's the code for John Wayne Airport in Orange County. Why I don't know. You'd think it would be JWN."

As she talked, I dug into my pocket and pulled out the mysterious note I'd found in my building, hoping the bullet didn't come flying out with it. "Does this mean anything to you?" I asked, handing the note to her.

"Well, five-twelve might be May twelfth, and SNA would be John Wayne Airport, like I said. TC probably means Terminal C, and G19 is likely Gate nineteen. The rest is obviously the time, ten-forty in the morning. This looks to me like a note telling someone when and where to pick somebody up at the airport. Did you find this in the rental?"

"No, no, I didn't."

"I hope whoever jotted this down made their connection."

Even if they did, it wouldn't be half as big as the connection I'd just made.

SIXTEEN

"You gonna tell me what that business with the slip of paper is all about?" Vince said when we were back in the limo.

"I found that note in my building right after finding Philly's body," I said, pulling the Caddy out onto the street. "It looked like someone had tried to throw it away and missed. My office address was written on the other side of the paper in the same handwriting. At least the numbers on both sides are written the same."

"So?"

"So whoever wrote it is connected to the murders."

"You mean the killer?"

"I'm not sure."

"Who, then?"

"Look, why would you write down flight information?"

"Because you need to pick someone up at the airport."

"Right. And then you write directions for a location...my office, as it turns out...where someone is murdered. What does that add up to?"

"Nothing that I can see," Vince said. "What do you think it adds up to?"

"I think it means the person flying into John Wayne may have been an out-of-town hit man."

"You're saying Philly got whacked by a torpedo?"

"I'm thinking out loud. But let's say whoever flew in, Mr. X for lack of a real name, was a hit man or a would-be-kidnapper hired to abduct you. But not long after he hits town you vanish on your own, upsetting his plans, as well as the person who hired him."

"Who hired him?"

"I don't know. Let's call him Mr. Y."

"Y?"

I don't know, he's on third, and I don't give a damn! I heard in my head but managed to keep from saying out loud.

"Mr. Y doesn't know you've taken off of your own volition," I went on. "He thinks Mr. X has you, so he sends the last ransom letter which implies you're being held. Then he finds out Mr. X has failed, and neither of them know where you are. But Philly does, because you called him. So they force the information out of Philly, then shoot him with his own gun, then track you down at the hotel in Mission Hills and follow you back to L.A., where they mistakenly take a shot at me, thinking it's you."

"Jesus, hold your horses, Beauchamp. What's this about Philly being shot with his own gun?"

"He was wearing a shoulder holster when I found him. An empty one. I can't prove he was shot with his own gun but it fits."

"No it doesn't, because Philly didn't carry a gun."

"He didn't?"

"He didn't. At least I never knew him to."

"Not even if he believed you were in danger?"

"Damn. You think my taking a powder caused the big *allocco* to start packing? Why would he do that?"

"If he finally confronted the person whom he believed had taken you, maybe he felt he could force the information out of him. Kind of ironic, isn't it?"

"I don't know what the hell it is," Vince moaned. "Nor do I know what any of this has to do with Annemarie getting killed."

"Well...that I don't know either. I'm hoping—"

"Hey, hang back a little. You're too close to the car in front. If it suddenly slams on the brakes, you're gonna rear-end him."

I hung back and then had to stop for another light. "You know, Vince, trying to think and talk while I'm driving this boat isn't easy. Can we stop for a little bit?"

"Little bit of what?"

"Can I pull over for a few minutes? I might make more sense when I'm not worried about the car."

"Okay, fine. You can't make much less sense."

There was a Ralphs grocery store a block up and I pulled into the parking lot. Sliding the limo into a parking spot was easier than I imagined, though it hung out several feet past the painted lines. "You don't need anything while we're here, do you?" I asked.

"Just tell me the rest of your speculation and then get me the hell home, okay?"

"Okay. Aside from the Annemarie connection, what I can't figure out is why Philly was in my office in the first place."

"Don't ask me. I had Philly drive me to your house one time, but even I don't know where your office is."

"It's on my business card. Didn't I give you one?"

"I don't remember. If you did I would have handed it over to Marnie."

He stopped and then looked up at me with fire in his eyes.

"Oh, no you don't," he said. "Don't even go there. Marnie had nothing to do with this."

"I'm not saying she did, though her involvement would answer a couple of the open questions."

"Like what?"

"Like what if the information as to your whereabouts wasn't forced out of Philly at gunpoint? What if he passed it on to someone he trusted implicitly? Someone who was just as worried about your welfare as he was...or at least seemed to be?"

"No, absolutely not! Marnie wouldn't have anything to do with this."

"But what if Philly called her and told her where you were, and she told him that she would call me, and we'd all meet in my office at a certain time. That would explain why he was there."

"You're saying *Marnie* is Mr. Y?" he cried. "You're saying she sent those letters then she hired a torpedo and picked him up at the airport, then what? When I disappear she has the torpedo kill Annemarie? And then she finds out where I am from Philly, kills him then comes after me again? Jesus Christ, Beauchamp, I haven't heard so much horseshit dropping since my last visit to Santa Anita!"

"The problem, Vince, is that the way you just explained it makes every puzzle piece fit into place," I said. "I hate to ask this as much as you're going to hate hearing it but, is there any reason Marnie would want both you and Annemarie out of the way?"

"Okay, this conversation is over. Take me home *now*, and after I'm there I don't ever want to see you or hear from you again! You got that?"

"Sorry Vince."

I started up the limo.

"Marnie's trying to kill me...horseshit! And you know what else? Your pieces *don't* fit. That business about her going to John Wayne airport on the twelfth, last Tuesday, that's garbage. She was at the plant all day Tuesday, not in Orange frigging–" He stopped yelling then. Much more quietly he muttered, "Oh, fuck me, I'm wrong. She got up early that morning and said she had to go to the office of our ad agency to look at a new campaign. She didn't get back until early afternoon."

"Where's your ad agency located?" I asked gently.

"Anaheim."

"Just up the freeway from John Wayne Airport."

"But I still don't buy it," he said. "I don't. I don't. The only reason she'd go to the airport would be to pick up...oh, no, no, no, uh-uh, no way Beauchamp, no fuckin' way!"

At first I didn't understand what he was protesting so vigorously, and then it hit me.

Who might be flying into town and need to be picked up at the airport by Vince, Marnie, or Philly?

His daughter Vickie.

"Look, Vince," I said, "I'm still trying to get a handle on all this. Anything I said, and any ideas I might have planted in your brain, are nothing but conjecture. I don't know anything for a fact yet, okay? I'm probably wrong. I've been wrong in the past."

"But you've been right, too. Jesus, what do I say when I get home?"

"Nothing about this. I'll come in with you and say something innocent but pointed, and see if Marnie has any reaction. Though I kind of wish my dad was here. He's really great at detecting subtle reactions in people's faces."

"Bring him along the next time."

"It'll be a while. He's having open heart surgery tomorrow."

"Jesus, Beauchamp, you should have said something. You should be worrying about him, not me."

"I am worrying about him, but that's about all I can do at the moment. I'll be at the hospital tomorrow."

"Which one?"

"Cedars."

"That's the place to be. I have several acquaintances who are members of the Zipper Club, and they're all doing great. So don't worry."

"Thanks, Vince."

Navigating the street that went up to his house in the Queen Mary seemed more difficult than descending the hill, but I managed. When we got, there the gate was closed.

"There's a little remote gizmo in a holder by the gear shift that opens the gate," Vince told me.

I found it and pressed the top button, and the stately iron barrier began to slide open. I drove up and let Vince out, then managed to get the boat inside the garage.

Inside we found Marnie and Paul with another man, whom I recognized from the picture that fell out of Vince's wallet.

"Hey, Mikey," he said, embracing his eldest son. "This guy is Dave Beauchamp. He's helping me out with some stuff."

"Oh, right," Michael said, offering his hand. "We spoke on the phone."

"Vickie phoned while you were gone," Marnie said. "She's on her way down."

"She's not here already?" I asked.

"I just said she was on her way down."

"Is she flying in? With everything you have going on, I could pick her up at the airport if that would help, though I hope it's not John Wayne."

Marnie's face remained perfectly placid, betraying nothing. "She's coming by train, but thanks anyway."

"Not a problem."

"You don't like John Wayne airport?" Michael asked.

"I got lost trying to get there one time," I lied. "I was supposed to meet someone at Terminal C and was over an hour late. They weren't happy."

I glanced at Marnie again, who now appeared to have tuned me out altogether. Then I casually looked over at Vince and very subtly shook my head. He seemed to get the message, for a look of relief crossed his face.

"Well, thanks, Beauchamp, for clearing up that business with the rental car," he said, starting to walk me toward the door. "And best of luck with your dad."

"Thanks. I'll be in touch."

As I was leaving I heard Michael asking, "What's all this about a rental car?" I figured Vince had some 'splainin' to do which would be better done without my interference.

After driving the limo, it seemed weird to get back into my Corolla. How quickly luxury corrupts one. I thought about stopping by Mom's house since I wasn't all that far away (by L.A. standards), but decided to let Hannah handle things. She seemed to be a little better at it.

Instead I swung by my office to see if it was still a crime scene.

Part of me was relieved to see it was not…at least there was no yellow tape blocking the door. But another part of me wished maybe the cops had let me know it was all right to go back in.

The door was locked which struck me as unusual since I'd never given the police a key.

Cautiously I opened it up and peeked in. It looked pretty much like it had the last time I was there, except there wasn't a human gorilla sitting dead in my chair. Entering I noticed the bloodstain in the seat. There was also dried blood on the floor.

How nice.

My phone machine light was blinking so I hit the button.

"Hi, Mr. Beauchamp," the recorded voice said, "this is Detective Lopez. I wanted to let you know we're through in your office. We used a device to lock the door behind us when we were done. You may want to call a crime scene cleanup company for the blood. We'll be in touch if we need you for anything else."

The call ended.

Knowing that both murderers and the police have the wherewithal to come and go in locked suites whenever they want did not instill a sense of security within me.

Examining the chair, I wondered if there were Yelp ratings for crime scene cleanup companies. Then again, the chair was most likely a goner and I could probably do the floor myself with a little spray cleaner.

Getting a flashlight out of my desk drawer, I inspected the hardwood more carefully to make sure the stain hadn't seeped through, making a bigger problem. Even if a professional inspection revealed it had, I wasn't going to need the office for much longer. I'd let the management company deal with it.

But that would wipe out my cleaning deposit, and twelve-hundred bucks was twelve-hundred bucks, inheritance or not.

Crouching down I examined the floor more closely. The blood spot was only borderline more disgusting than how filthy it was in general under the desk. On the bright side, I saw a quarter and a pencil lying there. I crawled under to get them, but in attempting to creep back out and rise to my feet, I managed to bash my head against the underside of my desk.

Hard.

A would-be murderer's bullet miraculously misses my head by centimeters so I manage to finish the job myself with my own furniture.

Welcome to Beauchampland.

Lying down on the floor, waiting for a little bit of the pain to subside, my gaze turned up to the bottom of my drawer.

I saw something.

Shining the light on it, pencil markings could be seen, perhaps made by the pencil I'd just found under the desk.

WW it read.

I had never written anything on the bottom of my drawer. Why would I? Either the marking was there when I bought the desk or someone else had made it. I carefully ran my finger across the letters and graphite rubbed off onto it. I'm no expert, of course, but if the marking was old, I don't think it would smear so easily.

Who could have written on the underside of my desk, and why?

Oh, come come! the voice of Basil Rathbone scolded inside my head. *You know perfectly well who.*

Philly Lepkowitz.

It was a dying clue, for crying out loud.

But what was the significance of *WW*?

Initials?

In his last seconds on earth had he recorded the identity of his killer?

If so, who was it?

Then it hit me.

"Oh, jeez," I muttered.

There was only one person connected with this mess that it could be.

SEVENTEEN

Pencil etchings on the bottom of a desk drawer, of course, would not stand up in court, but that would be *Wyatt Worsley's* problem. Why the head of Start Over Clinic would want to kill a former patient was certainly open for speculation, but I could speculate a solid half-dozen reasons right off the top of my battered head. High on the list was that something actually *had* happened to Annemarie at the clinic but not at the hands of Evan Sandburg…instead Worsley himself was the culprit. That would also explain why he seemed almost eager to see me immediately when I referenced her name. But if he was her killer, he certainly played it cool in front of us. Cold, calculated killers were not uncommon, though.

Since there was little more I could do here, I locked up and headed out to pick up some cleaner, and maybe an ice pack for my throbbing head.

Jeez, do they even make ice packs anymore?

If not, I'd buy a bag of frozen peas.

I was nearly inside the store market on the way home when my cell rang. I was beginning to wish Alexander Graham Bell had minded his own business.

It was Dane Colfax.

"No rest for the wicked, huh?" I answered.

"Unlike yesterday, I'm scheduled to work today," he replied. "I have something for you."

"Animosity?"

He chuckled. "Aside from that. I got the autopsy report on Annemarie Mazetta. They found something kind of weird."

"Drugs?"

"Well, yeah, but those aren't weird. We were actively looking for drugs. No, the M.E. discovered some cloth fibers in the ligature marks on her neck."

"What's weird about that?"

"Nothing. It confirms she was strangled with some sort of cloth. It's the other thing the M.E. found there that he can't explain."

"Go ahead and tell me. I'm ready for anything."

"Corn silk."

Except that.

"Corn silk?"

"You know, like you find on an ear of corn that's still in the husks."

"Yeah, I get it. But why corn silk?"

"If I could tell you that it wouldn't be weird. Since it is, I was hoping you'd have an idea."

"I'm afraid not. I've never heard of anyone dying from corn," I said.

You've never been to one of my performances, I heard the voice of Henny Youngman say.

"If you get any brilliant ideas, you'll let me know, right?"

"There's something I should pass on. I think I know who killed Philly Lepkowitz."

"Just happened to come to you, did it?"

"I found a dying clue in my office."

"A dying clue? You really have seen too many movies."

"Hear me out, Dane. There was a pencil on the floor under my office desk, which is where Philly died, and the initials WW were scratched out in pencil on the underside of my desk drawer. Those initials correspond to a guy named Wyatt Worsley, who's the head of Start Over Clinic in Malibu, which is where Annemarie Mazetta was a patient until fairly recently."

"Okay, you've got my interest now," Colfax said. "Do you know of any reason this Wyatt Worsley would want to kill Lepkowitz?"

"Possibly because Worsley also killed Annemarie to silence her about something bad that happened at the clinic that Philly knew about, so he had to be silenced too."

"You think Worsley used a silencer on the ear of corn he killed her with?"

"What?"

"Corn silk, Beauchamp, remember?"

"Oh, right."

"It's something, anyway. It's bug house crazy, of course, but still enough to warrant a visit to Mr. Worsley and tell my captain I've got a lead. Okay, Beauchamp, start over."

"Well…like I said, I found a pencil under my desk where Philly had been—"

"No, I'm writing down the name of the clinic! Start Over Clinic!"

"Oh, right. Sorry. It's in Malibu, just off Topanga Canyon Boulevard on a hilltop overlooking the ocean."

"Got it."

"You'll keep me posted about what you learn, won't you?"

"Don't I always? That's going to get me in hot water someday."

He cut off the call.

Corn silk. That simply didn't make sense.

Hannah was still gone when I got home, which didn't surprise me.

I was halfway through watching *I Wake Up Screaming*, which turned up on an antenna TV channel (yet another note to self: *Soon you'll be able to afford cable*), when she returned.

"Another of your films, eh?" she said, not in a judgmental way, as she sat down beside me.

"It's a classic of sorts," I said. "How's Mom?"

"About as well as can be expected. She's pretending to be brave but she's pretty frazzled. I did my best to reassure her."

"Good. I'm glad she has you. I'm glad I have you too, for that matter."

Hannah smiled and leaned over to kiss me. "But I thought you and I had agreed to not keep secrets from each other."

Had Mom informed her about the divorce? "What do you mean?"

"I told you about my brother Christian, right?"

"Yeah."

"So why didn't you tell me you had a sister?"

Had an anvil stamped with the brand name *Acme* fallen on my head at that moment, I doubt I could have been more stunned.

"A...sister? I don't have a sister. I'm an only child."

"Your mom said they had a little girl before you were born, but she died." My face must have told the entire story because Hannah said, "You didn't know, did you?"

"This is the first time I've ever heard about any kind of sibling."

"Oh, wow. Well, I guess this is Ma Beauchamp's way of telling you through me. She was born in 1979, your sister I mean, but only lived a couple weeks. They think she had an intestinal problem and couldn't absorb food."

"Good lord. Now it makes sense why Mom hates the thought of me being put in any kind of danger. My whole life, they never said a word."

"She said they didn't think you needed to know."

"Did she happen to mention if my sister had a name?"

"Kellie," Hannah said. "She's buried in a cemetery in Westwood, if you ever want to go see her."

"I wouldn't know what to say," I muttered.

What I really did not know how to say was that, if not for Hannah, I would have never learned about this.

My mom accepted her as family before accepting me.

My head started hurting again.

I tried to focus on tomorrow. Dad's surgery was scheduled for eight in the morning, which put the kibosh to my plan to drop his files off in Century City beforehand. But I doubted another day would make much difference. Or even several days.

Mr. Cleerman won't be any less guilty or innocent by Friday.

Since Hannah had been cooking for Mom pretty much all day, preparing food to package up for the rest of the week, I recommended we go out for dinner. It didn't take much convincing to get her to agree.

While waiting for our food at the coffee shop diner, I sprung the question...not *that* question; our getting married was already settled. I asked Hannah what she thought about trading in her Mini Cooper for a bigger car.

"But that car was Mr. Hanley's," she said.

"I know, but it's a little small for the two of us," I countered. "Plus, I drove Vince Mazetta's Cadillac limousine and I have to say it was pretty sweet."

"Then why don't you get rid of your car and buy a limousine?"

"Not a bad idea," I said, figuring I could donate the Corolla to the local public television station that showed classic films every Friday night. "If I were to do that, I guess we could use that car whenever we travel together, and then you could keep the Mini just for you."

"Seems fair," she said.

After dinner, we returned home and did very little since both of us were weary from the week's roller coaster excitement. Since tomorrow was going to be no less stressful, I turned in early hoping to get a few solid hours of sleep before getting up at the crack of dawn to get to the hospital. I doubted that would be the case, but I can dream, can't I?

EIGHTEEN

The alarm went off at six but I was already up.

No matter how many assurances one has from the professionals, trying to rest when you know a loved one is scheduled to have his chest cut open and his heart exposed is nearly impossible.

Hannah and I were out the door by 6:30 and made it to Cedars with plenty of time to spare.

Mom was not in the lobby, so I had to assume she was in Dad's room.

We made it there just in time to see him being wheeled out, heading for pre-op.

"Hey, Davy, you made it," he said, wanly.

"Of course."

"How are you, darling?" he asked Hannah.

"Fine. Just like you're going to be later today."

We followed Dad down the hall to the elevator, and just as the door opened, he said, "Just in case it doesn't turn out that way, you'll have to be around for the paperwork, Davy."

Desperation being the mother of invention (and fear the father), I suddenly had a brain flash. "Hey, Dad," I blurted out, "How many Goldwyn Girls does it take to screw in a light bulb?"

"I have no idea. How many?"

"I'll tell you after the operation. See you later."

The elevator door closed.

"What was that all about?" Mom asked.

"I'm hoping he'll be so curious to find out the answer that he'll be determined to sail through the procedure," I said.

"That was pretty clever," Hannah said.

"You can tell me how many Goldwyn Girls it takes to screw in a light bulb," Mom said. "I'm not going into surgery."

I looked at her and smiled. "I don't know, I just made it up on the spot. Sudden inspiration. But I've got a few hours to come up with an answer."

"What are Goldwyn Girls anyway?" Hannah asked.

"They were dancers in movies produced by Sam Goldwyn."

"Why would it take more than one to screw in a light bulb? Oh, wait, is this a dirty joke?"

"No, it's actually a common set up for a gag. Like…How many mystery writers does it take to screw in a light bulb? Two…one to screw it in most of the way and the other to give it a final surprising twist."

Hannah smiled but didn't laugh.

"For now," I said, "I suggest we find the cafeteria and see what's for breakfast."

After seeing it, we opted to strike out and look for a nearby eatery on the street. The best bet appeared to be a café that offered breakfast croissants. We squeezed ourselves into a tiny corner table and ordered.

Just after the food and tea came, my phone rang.

"I don't believe it," I muttered, looking at the screen. I didn't recognize the number.

"Dave Beauchamp," I said into the device.

"Mr. Beauchamp, I'm calling from Cedars," the female voice said. "Are you still in the hospital?"

"Is something wrong?" I asked, and saw both Mom and Hannah stiffen.

"No, no, nothing's wrong. We simply need you to fill out some paperwork that I thought had already been done."

"Oh. We're at a café across the street. Does it have to be done immediately?"

"When you come back is fine."

"What kind of paperwork is it?"

"Organ donor paperwork."

I groaned.

"It's purely a formality. We have everyone sign, just in case. They should have brought it to you while you were on the floor."

"I'm glad they didn't. We'll be back within a half-hour, is that all right?"

"Fine. Just go to the nursing desk on the sixth floor, and it will be waiting for you."

I hung up and saw both Mom and Hannah staring at me apprehensively.

"What?" Mom asked.

"Nothing, just some paperwork. A formality."

"Harvesting his organs, right?"

"Um…yeah."

"Mm-hmm. They brought it to me and I told them you had to decide."

"Okay, I guess I'll leave his heart to San Francisco."

I had not meant it to sound snarky. In fact, I had not meant it to come out of my mouth at all. But some time back it was pointed out to me that tense, even dangerous situations bring out glibness in me not normally there.

"If you're going to do that," Mom said, "send his kidney to Sydney, too."

"Or his spleen to Aberdeen," I countered.

She laughed.

"Or his eyes to Van Nuys."

Now I laughed.

"As long as we're there, let's float his spine down the Rhine."

"And send his brain to Fort Wayne."

"And maybe his sinus to the Carolinas."

Now Hannah was looking back and forth between us not knowing exactly what to do or say. Finally she offered: "How about his bladder to Nevada?"

Mom and I lost it then, and before long all three of us were laughing uncontrollably. The server showed up at our table and said, "Must've been a good one."

"We're vivisecting my father!" I cried, and the three of us howled again.

It took several minutes to regain control.

"They're going to throw us out of here, you know," Mom said.

"I hope they do it before the bill arrives," I said.

The server brought the bill a minute later with an expression that indicated: *Okay, I know a con when I see one and you're not getting away with it.*

I left her a good tip.

As we walked back to the hospital, Mom said, "Heaven help me, I needed that."

"We all did," I replied.

Back up on the sixth floor, I asked for the paperwork.

"Sorry about this, sir," the nurse receptionist said as I signed the form, "it's just a formality."

"I understand. Just make certain his tooth goes to Duluth, okay?"

Then I turned and walked away without waiting for a reaction.

None of us said much for the next couple hours. I read the newspaper, absorbing little of it, Mom read the book she'd brought with her, and after a while Hannah announced she was going to take a stroll around the hospital.

"What are you hoping to see?" I asked.

"Oh, I might stop in and say hi to people if they look lonely."

When she was gone, I told Mom, "She's got something of an addiction to helping people, doesn't she?"

"Yes, she does. She was completely devoted to Palmer Hanley, who was a really great old guy even though he inadvertently started a titanic con scheme. I think it helps her feel worthy."

It took me another several minutes before I was able to say, "Mom, Hannah told me about Kellie."

She dropped her head down. "And now you're angry with me again, right?"

"No, not angry. Just a bit shocked. And saddened."

"We didn't want to tell you because…well, I didn't want to relive the experience, I suppose. It almost overwhelmed your father. You've no idea what losing a child is like."

"You're right. I don't. Do you ever visit her?"

"At the cemetery? No. I did before you were born. Not since. But I still dream about her sometimes. I probably always will."

I took her hand and went silent again.

It was getting close to lunchtime when Dr. Metcalf suddenly appeared in the waiting area. Mom and I both jumped up.

"How is he?" Mom asked.

"Well, it could have gone better," he said, "but I don't see how."

Both of us sounded like locomotive engines letting off excess steam.

"Carl came through like a champ. He'll be in recovery for a while and then taken to the CCU, where he'll be under constant observance. Even though it's a pretty common procedure, we don't take chances."

"When can we see him?" I asked.

"If everything goes as well as we expect, you might be able to see him tomorrow, though briefly. Call first, and don't catch a cold between now and then or we won't be able to let you in."

"So you won't be able to finish your joke," Mom said to me.

"Sorry, you've lost me," Dr. Metcalf said.

I told him of my sudden inspiration to make up a stupid joke but not reveal the punch line until after the operation, in hopes of raising his incentive to pull through. "Kind of a dumb idea, I guess," I said.

"No, not at all," the doctor replied. "Rather ingenious in a way, in fact. What was the set-up?"

"How many Goldwyn Girls does it take to screw in a light bulb? A Goldwyn Girl is a chorus dancer in old movies."

"I know. My grandmother used to be one."

"Really? Is she still with us?"

Metcalf smiled. "Yes, she's eighty-seven. She came in toward the end of Goldwyn's career, but was in *Walter Mitty* and *Guys and Dolls*. So tell me, how many Goldwyn Girls *does* it take to screw in a light bulb?"

"That's the thing," I muttered. "I haven't figured it out yet."

"How about none?" Metcalf said. "They prefer dancing in the dark."

"I like it," I told him.

"Why don't you give him the answer, doctor?" Mom suggested.

"If he asks about it and it looks like he won't rest until he knows, I'll pass it on. Otherwise I'll leave it to you. The best thing you could do now is go home and rest, and leave the healing to us. You can always check in by phone. I have to get back now, but try not to worry."

"How?" Mom asked.

"By acknowledging that everything went as well as it could have, and worrying won't make a bit of difference in Carl's recovery. So be easy on yourself."

"Thanks, doctor," I said, as he headed back for the elevator. "Mom, do you need Hannah to go back home with you?"

"No, I'll be fine. Even if Carl bounces right back to his normal self after this, the hard truth is one of us is going to leave the other someday, permanently. This is a way to try and get used to the idea. Besides, I'd like to go home now and she's still making her rounds. Tell her I said goodbye."

"All right. Call if you need anything."

"Boy. I'm not used to hearing you say that."

"I'm not used to saying it, but this is the new normal, right?"

"Right."

She gave me a hug and then walked out of the lobby without looking back.

I sat for another forty-five minutes, rereading the newspaper, before Hannah returned. "Where's Ma Beauchamp?" she asked.

"She went home. The doctor came down and said everything went great, and maybe we can see Dad tomorrow."

"I'll check in with Felicia and see how he's doing."

"Who's Felicia?"

"The head nurse on six. We talked for a while."

Once we got home Hannah made a beeline for the bathroom. "Too much ice tea at that restaurant," she said.

I used the alone-time to pull out the number given to me by Colleen-Who-Looked-Like-Maureen and my phone, and gave her a ring. "Hi, this is Dave Beauchamp," I said after hearing her machine beep. "Dad's operation went extremely well. He'll be in the hospital for several more days but could probably take calls by tomorrow, maybe. Only family can visit while he's in the CCU, though. Once he gets to a private room, you can visit. You might want to call first, though, and ask the nurse on duty if he's seeing anyone at that moment, because there's a good chance it would be my mom. If it's me, don't worry. Bye."

Then I remembered I still needed to take Dad's legal files to his office, where I probably could ask to see Colleen face-to-face.

Oh, well.

It was after two now, and the day-long traffic jam (formerly known as rush hour) would be in full force between here and Century City, so I decided to put it off until tomorrow. I did, however, put in a call to Len Allen to pass along Dad's condition and let him know he was relinquishing the cases, and that I'd be in mid-morning to drop the stuff off.

While we were trying to figure out what to do with the rest of the day, Hannah's cell phone rang. That was unusual because she took pains not to give her cell number out. Probably fewer than six people had it. Glancing at the screen, she said, "It's Mr. Neale."

Richard Neale, our attorney.

Hannah listened for a minute, and then said, "I think so, but let me check. Dave, would it be all right if Mr. Neale dropped by later today?"

"Here?"

"That's what he said. He has something important to tell us."

"Real lawyers actually make house calls?"

She held out the phone. "Do you want to talk to him?"

I took it.

"Oh, hi, Dave," he said. "I was asking Hannah if I might be able to swing by a little later. I've got a dinner event this evening at the Sportsmen's Lodge and since you're just down the street, I thought I'd swing by beforehand and save you a trip to the office."

"Sure, that would be all right."

"I think you'll like some of the news I'm bringing with me."

"But not all of it?"

"I can't predict. But I'll see you in a bit and fill you in on what's happening."

After we disconnected, Hannah said, "What's going on?"

"I'm not sure, but it must be important. He said he'd have news we liked and some we might not."

The next three hours weren't the longest I've experienced, but they didn't go by in a flash, either.

Richard Neale buzzed the front to be let in a little after five.

He was dressed to the nines, so whatever event he had scheduled later must be a semi-formal one.

"Getting an award this evening?" I asked as a joke when he came into the apartment.

"Actually, yes," he replied. "But not for lawyering. My tennis club is having their annual dinner, and I'm getting some kind of certificate for being an all-around swell guy, and also sponsoring a junior golf league for kids. But, that's neither here nor there."

He took a seat on the sofa and opened his briefcase, pulling out some paperwork. "The news I know you will be happy to hear is that probate closed and your inheritance will be wired to your bank accounts this Friday. As you know that comes to one and one-half million to you, Hannah, and one million to you, Dave. I strongly encourage you to open up new savings accounts at any bank of your choice, at your earliest convenience, to receive the transfers. Do it tomorrow if possible. Once you have done so, please forward to me the account information so I can facilitate the transfers."

"Can't we simply open up one joint account?" I asked.

"It would be better for you to keep your inheritances separate for a variety of reasons," Neale replied. "And they should be savings accounts, not checking."

"But we will still have access to the money, right?" Hannah asked.

"Of course. It's simply that an interest-bearing account will do exactly that and earn you more money."

"So what's the bad news?" I asked. "The tax bite?"

"No, you're in the clear on that since your inheritance is under five-million. Congratulations. Maybe I should have said *complicating* news instead of bad news. I know the two of you are planning to be married."

"That's right, though we haven't set a date yet."

"Don't," the lawyer said.

"What?" Hannah gasped.

"Do not get married, at least not yet. My office has received letters from the legal team representing that outfit both you, Hannah, and Palmer Hanley were a part of for a while, the Temple of…I can never pronounce it."

"Theotologics," I prompted.

"Right. In a rather clever move on their part—from a purely legal standpoint, mind you—they decided not to contest the will during probate in favor of suing you for the money once you've received it, on the grounds that Palmer Hanley was not in his right mind and was influenced by you to change his will."

"That's not true," Hannah said.

"I know it's not true," Neale said. "I knew Palmer. The point is, purely in legal terms, they can make the case. They plan to focus on you and your inheritance, Hannah, since you knew Palmer for such a long time. That's why you should have separate accounts. If your combined inheritances are in one account, that would be the amount at risk. In separate accounts, however, they would have to file two separate suits, and that's where their case starts to look like a clear exercise in greed."

"There's no way they can win, is there?" I asked.

Neale shrugged. "In my opinion, this is a totally frivolous suit based on a spurious claim, and should be recognized immediately as such, given the Temple's history. However, I am not the judge. I cannot promise that the case, should it go to trial, would not be ruled in their favor. That's why it's a diabolically-clever move. And that's why you need to hold off on the wedding, so your individual accounts cannot be construed to be a joint account."

"For how long?"

Neale shrugged again.

"Like I said before, I see this as nothing but a cynical play for cash that they don't deserve, and I plan to fight it on that basis every step of the way. The best case scenario is that it gets thrown out of court upon first hearing. That would be the ideal. Worst case scenario is it actually goes to trial, you lose, which means you appeal, which means the case will drag on and on potentially for years until one side blinks and a settlement is reached."

"But in the meantime we can't get married," Hannah said.

"Please understand me," Neale responded, "there is nothing legally saying you *cannot* get married whenever you want. I am simply arguing against it as a way of protecting your assets. Having been married twice, I suppose I could be accused of erring on the side of assets."

Hannah looked at me with a pleading expression, and said, "Dave?"

"Mr. Neale," I began, "if you're asking us to choose between love and money, I would personally vote for love."

"Very well," he said.

"But I might vote twice for doing whatever it takes to not let the bastards get away with stealing from us." I went to Hannah and took her hand. "Not having a piece of paper doesn't mean we're not in love. Since we haven't gotten around to finding a date yet, maybe we simply put it off for a little longer and see what happens. At least until next month. Think we can do that?"

Hannah nodded. "I hope that your folks won't be disappointed, though," she said. "I hope the two of us living together for a while without being married won't bother them."

"Oh…I think they might understand a situation like that," I said.

She smiled. "I guess you know them better than I do."

Or so I thought.

After Dick Neale left to go off to his event, Hannah brought up the subject of our own dinner. I'd forgotten we hadn't eaten anything since the croissants at that little café by the hospital. "What have we got?" I asked.

"I've been kind of hungry for spaghetti," she replied, "but I don't know if we have everything for it."

"I could go to the store."

After taking stock of our canned goods, Hannah realized we had no jars of sauce or tomato soup. "That's my secret ingredient," she said, "the soup. Oh, and get an onion, too."

I continued to fantasize about owning a limousine, or maybe just a town car, all the way to the grocery store. Once inside I got everything Hannah requested and also looked around for other things we might need to go with the spaghetti. Some nice, warm bread sounded good, so I stuck a crusty, yard-long baguette in my cart.

In the checkout line I was behind a woman who was buying ears of corn, and suddenly I became fixated by the sight of it. It was not that I wanted fresh corn along with the pasta; it was that corn silk had been found on the neck of Annemarie Mazetta. Looking at the three reusable shopping bags she brought with her reminded me that I had left my one at home.

Had I been driving Vince's limo, all I would have had to do was get the one from the trunk, which contained the…

"Oh…oh, no," I muttered. "It can't be…can it?"

I reached for my cell phone, where I had Vince Mazetta's number on speed dial.

A voice from somewhere asked, "Do you have a rewards card?"

It was the checkout clerk.

"Oh, yes." I managed to fish out my store card for the clerk. "I'll need a bag, too," I said, "Paper's fine."

Through the phone I heard Vince's recorded voice say: *You've called the Mazetta residence…Leave a message when you hear the tone, but only if it's real.*

Of course he wasn't at home. He'd still be at the office.

I clicked off and tried the number for Perfect Friends.

"Sir, that will be nine-forty-three," the clerk said impatiently.

"What?"

"Good afternoon, Perfect Friends Pet Foods," the voice of the receptionist said through the phone."

"Hi, I need to speak to Marnie," I said. "It's important."

"Hold on, sir."

I could hear the guy in line behind me, an older man wearing a ball cap, mutter impatiently, "Would you put the damn phone away and pay?"

"Oh, sorry," I said to the clerk. "How much?"

In unison I heard: "Nine-forty-three" and "This is Marnie."

"Marnie, it's Dave, I need you to check something for me."

"Sir?" the clerk prompted.

"This is the goddamn express lane," the man in the ball cap grumbled.

I pulled out my wallet and handed her a bill.

"Do you have anything smaller?" she asked.

"What do you need me to check?" Marnie asked, as the guy behind me started staring at the ceiling.

"Hold on, Marnie." I set the phone down while I fished out a twenty, taking back the hundred I'd originally handed the clerk.

"Okay, I'm back," I said, while the clerk counted out my change and then started bagging my order.

"Dave, what's going on?"

"Did you have corn on the cob at any point in the last week?"

"Did I...what?"

"Have a good evening," the clerk said, handing me the receipt.

I grabbed the bag, cleared the cart from the aisle and said, "I asked if you had corn on the cob recently."

"What kind of question is that?"

"A very important one. Please tell me."

"Yes, we had corn a few days ago while Vince was gone. Philly had dinner here. In fact, I think he bought the corn. I sent him to the store to get him out of my hair."

Oh, lord.

"Now, there's something I need you to do for me," I went on. "Did Vince take his limo to work today?"

"Yes. With Philly gone, I drove him in this morning. Why?"

"I need you to check the trunk of the limo and see if there's a grocery store shopping bag in it."

"Dave, have you been drinking?"

"Please check for me."

"You want me to go all the way down to the parking lot and check the trunk? Is this some kind of Mafia joke? Because if it is, I'm not really in the mood."

"It's no joke. I need to know. It might be a break in the case."

"Jesus. Okay. Hold on."

The impatient man behind me in the checkout line wheeled his cart past, glared at me, and shook his head. I smiled back.

After another couple minutes Marnie came back on the line.

"To answer your question, no, there is no bag of any kind. I found three bottles of motor oil, some glass cleaner, a satchel, and some other stuff. Now, would you like to tell me what this is all about?"

"You're not going to like, it," I said, and then told her what I suspected. I was not at all surprised by her reaction.

"Are you nuts?" Marnie cried. "You think *Philly* killed Annemarie?"

"The medical examiner found traces of a cloth fiber and corn silk on Annemarie's neck. I couldn't figure out how corn silk would get on a cloth until I went to the store, where I am right now, actually, and the lady in line in front of me was buying ears of corn, which were put into her shopping bag. I realized how easy it would be to strangle someone with the straps of a cloth grocery bag, which is such a common item that millions of people in L.A. probably have one. Then I remembered that Philly was one of those millions. Right after Vince went missing, I looked in the limo trunk and saw such a bag there, which you say is no longer there. "

"Look, Dave, just because we ate corn a few days ago, and there's no shopping bag in the car, doesn't mean Philly killed Annemarie. I mean, that's something of a leap of logic."

"Agreed. But it's a leap that ties all the strange clues together. Philly had a bag in the trunk. He buys corn, which means some of the silk could have gotten stuck on the straps. For some reason he's carrying the bag when he meets Annemarie and uses it to kill her, then gets rid of the evidence, which is why the bag is no longer in the car."

"How do you know he met her?"

"I don't. All I'm saying is that I can give this to the police as a lead to check out. They still have Annemarie's clothing and whatever jewelry she might have been wearing. They can check them for latent prints to see if any match Philly's."

"What if Philly's prints aren't in the system?"

"*Philly's* in the system, Marnie. He's still in the morgue. Taking his prints will not be a problem."

"I can't believe Philly would murder anyone," she said.

"Could you believe he didn't intend to?" I asked. "Is it possible he accidentally killed someone not knowing his own strength?"

There was a long pause before she whispered, "I saw Philly pick up the back of the limo one time so a tire jack could be put under it, so yes, it's possible. But why? Why would he even want to threaten Annemarie?"

"My guess is because Annemarie was somehow threatening Vince."

"Shit. Am I supposed to tell this to him? I don't know how he'd accept the theory that his trusted employee murdered his ex-wife."

"Don't tell Vince yet. Let me call my friend at Robbery-Homicide and fill him in, and then see what he discovers. If my theory proves to be all wet, then we don't have to say anything to anyone."

"But you think it's possible?"

"It's worth considering."

"You'd have to show me videotape of Philly actually murdering someone before I fully accept it," she said. "Besides, how does this factor into Philly's murder?"

"I think I know, Marnie, but I'm asking you to trust me a little longer regarding that."

Annemarie Mazetta, the former charge of Wyatt Worsley, is killed by Philly who wrote Worsley's initials on the bottom of my desk drawer.

It had to add up.

It had to.

Didn't it?

NINETEEN

I might not be the best PI in L.A., but I'm one of the cleanest. I was in the shower the next day when my phone rang.

"Dave, Copper's on the phone," Hannah said through the curtain.

He was returning the call I'd left for him last evening: a detailed message that was part apology for phoning yet again, but mostly laying out my suspicions and asking him to follow up on the information before it was too late…in other words, before Annemarie and Philly were buried.

I toweled off enough to not drip on the phone.

"Beauchamp, your hunches are getting better," Colfax said by way of hello. "I handled things personally as soon as I got your message. I had the morgue take prints from Lepkowitz and they perfectly match a latent found on a brass bracelet the Mazetta woman was wearing. We're still checking on the cloth fibers found on her neck, but the fingerprint takes precedent over that. It's a good thing he wasn't wearing gloves."

"I don't think he intended to kill her, Dane, I think it just happened," I said. "The bigger question is…why he was even with her?"

"Obviously, we can't ask. But simply having a suspect is going to make my captain happy. So if you get any other good hunches, call me back. If they stink, though, keep them to yourself."

He hung up.

Once I was dressed, I called the hospital and was put through to the coronary care unit. "Your father's doing well," the nurse told me. "He's sleeping at present and probably will for most of the day. He's still a little weak but that's to be expected. He's not up for visitors quite yet, but I'll be sure to tell him you called when he wakes up."

I thanked her and crossed that off my list for the day.

Following Richard Neale's advice, Hannah and I went to the bank and opened the separate savings accounts. The teller could not quite understand why we did not open a joint one and I did not feel like explaining. I merely said, "This is the way we want it, at least for the time being," and explained that both accounts would soon be getting substantial amounts wired to them.

Since Hannah was not interested in accompanying me on the rest of my planned errands, I dropped her off back at the apartment. Taking whatever cleaning sprays I found under the kitchen sink and a roll of paper towels, as well as Dad's files, I headed back out.

Stopping first at my office, I was happy to see the phone message light was not blinking. Unfortunately, I had waited a little too long to clean up the blood, since the floor and chair were buzzing with flies.

Opening my office window, I tried to shoo out as many as I could, and sprayed the rest.

Sorry, guys, but you weren't invited.

How the heck did they even get in here?

It took about a half-hour to clean everything up. I put the cleaner-and-blood-stained paper towels into the trashcan and set it in my office chair, which I wheeled down to the dumpster behind the building. After emptying the can, I picked up the chair to chuck it in. It was heavier than it looked, but I managed.

Going back up, I took a long look at the office I'd inhabited for three years now, but would soon be abandoning. I'd have to figure out what to do with the desk and the tiny fridge. The fridge I could simply leave for the next tenant. The desk I wanted to take with me, even though it would cramp the apartment. I also wanted to hang onto that cheesy painting of a moody, rainy streetscape that I could never get to hang straight. Going to the wall, I attempted for the umpteenth time to straighten it, gave up, and instead took it down and carried it out with me. Placing it in the back seat of my Corolla, I headed to my dad's Century City office, parking once again at the mall and hiking to the building.

It took only a minute, after announcing my presence in the reception area of Allen, Garbedian and Lomax, for Len Allen to emerge from the office labyrinth.

He practically ran toward me.

"Dave!" he cried, holding out his hand. "I'm so glad you came. We've not been able to get much information about Carl's condition."

"He had the operation yesterday and is doing as well as can be expected," I said. "But he's not going to be returning to work any time soon, if at all."

"Oh. Oh, dear."

"I brought these files back so you can reassign them to other attorneys."

"Yes, yes, thank you," he said, taking them and setting them on the receptionist's desk. "You really think he's going to retire?"

"I'm not sure he wants to, but it might be moot. It will take some time before he's even up to making that decision, I'm afraid."

"I see. Well, you know everyone here is rooting for a speedy recovery."

"Thank you. As long as I'm here maybe I should go to his office and pack up his personal things, just in case."

"I believe they're already in storage," the young male receptionist behind him chimed in.

"His stuff's already been packed up and moved out?" I asked.

"You must understand that office space here is rather at a premium," Allen replied, shooting a withering glare at the receptionist for letting the cat out of the bag. "Mr. Weller, why don't you call for Mr. Beauchamp's belongings to be retrieved from storage and brought up here."

The poor guy was visibly shaking from Allen's visual rebuke and punched the wrong button in his first attempt.

Turning back to me, Allen said, "Thank you for coming in, Dave. Please continue to keep us updated." Then he dashed back into the rabbit warren of hallways and cubicles and disappeared.

"I'm sorry about your father," Weller said. "I always liked him, which is more than I can say for everybody around here."

"Thanks," I said.

It took about twenty minutes for two bankers' boxes crammed with photos, statuettes, awards, and a few books to appear in the reception lobby, time I killed by sitting on a small sofa and watching a constant loop of Allen, Garbedian and Lomax mini-documentaries on a closed circuit television.

I noticed Dad didn't appear in any of them, though Len Allen was the star of each one.

The workman who had dollied the boxes up was good enough to take them back down to the lobby.

"Just leave them here and I'll go get my car," I said.

"I can't simply leave them," he replied. "Where are you parked?" After learning, he volunteered to accompany me straight to my car. "I don't get the chance to leave the salt mine very often," he explained.

Once the boxes were packed into the Corolla, I held out my hand to him and thanked him. Taking the hand truck, he slowly headed back to the office building.

On the way back home I wondered how Hannah would react to my wanting to keep the painting, but since she was out when I got there, I couldn't ask. I doubted she'd object, though, since I'd put up no argument about housing Palmer's remains.

Still in a pensive mood, I wandered around the empty apartment knowing that we would soon be vacating it. Dealing with so many changes in one's life all at once was not so much a case of abandoning old friends as removing the levels of comfort it had taken years to build up. This apartment may not be much but it was comfortable. The same went for my office. Even my car.

In its own way, the thought of abandoning all of that for as yet unknown replacements was as disconcerting as being shot at.

Yes, I know, but it is all part of life's rich pageant, the voice of Inspector Clouseau said inside my head.

Hannah finally arrived carrying a shopping bag filled with cleaning supplies.

"You took everything we had with you, so I got some more," she said. "We needed a few other things, too. What's all this stuff?"

"Dad's belongings from his office," I said. "I'm going to deliver them to the house next time we go over. Except for this." I held up the painting. "This is from my office, and I'd kind of like to keep it."

After setting down her bag, she came over to examine it. "I guess I could deal with looking at this every day, if it means that much to you."

"It's weirdly sentimental."

"Like me and Mr. Palmer's Mini." She pointed at the small figure in the painting making his way down the rainy street. "Ever wonder who that is?"

"I never really thought about it. Someone with his own life, his own problems that he's dealing with, but we'll never know, I guess."

How long had I been looking at this painting without really looking at it? I suddenly wondered. *How long had I been living my life without really living it?*

"Go ahead and put it up," she said, "and if I get tired of looking at it, we can hang it upside down. Then it will be like modern art."

I grinned, wondering if hanging it upside down would make it hang any straighter.

At a little after five I called the hospital again and this time Dad was awake enough to talk, though he sounded very weak.

"Hey, Davy," he drawled. "I talked to your mom just a little bit ago. She seems to be holding up all right."

"It's been very stressful for her. For all of us, in fact. But Hannah's been helping her out at home."

"That's a good filly you've corralled, Pilgrim," Dad said through an appalling John Wayne impersonation.

"I know."

"Hey, the doctor told me the answer to that joke of yours, the one about the Goldwyn Girls. Did you know his grandmother was a Goldwyn Girl?"

"He said something about that."

"The thing is "Dancing in the Dark' wasn't from a Goldwyn movie, it was from *The Band Wagon*. MGM."

"I guess I was misinformed," I said in an equally bad Bogart.

Bad doesn't begin to describe it, kid, Bogie commented inside my head.

"I took those files back to your firm today," I went on. "Len Allen sends his best. I let him know, though, that it would probably be a while before you came back to work. If at all."

"Good," he said. "Funny how when they give you the knock-out juice, and you're down to your last few seconds of consciousness, which might be your last few seconds *period*, you realize there's more important things than putting on a necktie every day and defending accused rapists."

"Well, the law is important, Dad."

"Yes it is, but the law was there before I entered the bar and it will go on after I'm done with it."

"Here's another one for you," I said, suddenly inspired. "John Barrymore, W.C. Fields, and Errol Flynn enter the bar. Which one leaves first?"

"That's simple...the one easiest to carry."

We shared a laugh, which on his end turned into another coughing jag.

"Okay, okay," I heard him say. "The nurse is signaling me to wrap things up, Davy."

"All right, Dad. I'll get up to see you soon."

"You do that."

I clicked off my cell with a real sense of helplessness. Dad was in the best hands, but there was nothing I could do for him. Just like Philly was dead, and there was nothing I could do for him.

Except catch his killer, the raked gravel voice of Charles McGraw said inside my head.

Right.

It was likely the stress of the day that caused me to turn in early, only a little after nine. Hannah was watching television.

I had no problem falling asleep, but the dreams started early.

I was walking down that dark, rainy street in the painting, following the shadow in front of me. No matter how fast I walked, the shadow remained the same distance ahead. I began to run and it disappeared.

Then the street changed to my office, only a much larger, much nicer version of my office, with better furniture.

Maybe I was the man in that painting, having just stepped out.

The overhead light was burnt out, and suddenly the replacement bulb was in my hand. Rather than standing on a chair or the desk to reach it, I simply leapt in the air and stayed there, easily fixing the light with no means of support.

I'd had flying dreams before and I always liked them. This one was no different.

After hovering about my desk for a minute, I actually set foot on the ceiling and stood there, upside down, before the office changed into Ventura Boulevard, but a fantasy version of it that was all but devoid of people and cars. I rose into the air again, this time soaring to the tops of the buildings, peddling my legs like I was on an invisible bicycle to remain aloft.

Then I started to fall.

Then I woke up with the sensation of bouncing on the bed, as though I had fallen from a rooftop and landed on the mattress.

This had happened to me before. In fact, I've heard it's a fairly common sleep phenomenon. There was once an urban legend stating that if you fell out of bed at the moment of impact in your dream and hit the floor, the shock would kill you. I believed that until I started thinking about it and wondered how it was possible to know that? If someone falls out of bed and dies, how could anyone know what they were dreaming moments before? They're dead, they can't tell you.

After I stopped "bouncing," I realized that my dream had been a sleep reaction to Hannah's comment about hanging the painting upside down.

In my experience, dreams always had a reason.

I rolled over and tried to get back to sleep again.

Then my eyes flew open and I sat upright, just like in the movies.

"Upside down," I muttered.

Unless I was crazy...I now knew who had killed Philly Lepkowitz.

TWENTY

Were this a movie, I'd gather all the suspects in a room and launch into the long process of laying out the evidence as I strode up and down among them, describing how I arrived at my conclusions as to which one present was the killer. But this wasn't a movie. Even so, the suspects were already scheduled to be gathered together in a room, and who am I to let a good opportunity fly out the window?

Annemarie Mazetta's funeral was scheduled for Thursday morning at St. Martin of Tours Catholic Church in Brentwood. Even though Hannah had nothing to do with this investigation or the people involved, she asked to accompany me, just so she could see the wrap-up of my final case. As long as she was going, I asked her to keep a close watch on the mourners as I did my thing.

After spending most of Wednesday struggling to convince Dane Colfax to go along with my plan, I got up early the day-of, put on my best suit (by which I mean my only suit) and left early in anticipation of bad traffic. We made it to the church fifteen minutes early.

As I parked in the lot, I noticed a car at the far end and recognized the driver.

"Do you want to say hi to Detective Colfax before we go in?" I asked Hannah.

"Sure."

We strolled over to his parked car. Dane was reading the *Times* and sipping from a Starbuck's cup.

"Hey, Copper," Hannah said.

Lowering his sunglasses, Colfax said, "Hey, Red. Are you going to be part of this little drama too?"

"An extra pair of eyes," I answered for her. "I don't see any police backup."

I wasn't expecting cruisers, but I thought there might be come plain-clothes officers.

"You're not supposed to see them," Colfax said. "And if I haven't stated so yet, you'd better be right about this, Beauchamp."

"The more I've thought about this the more pieces have fallen into place. It's the only answer."

Boy, I hoped I was right.

A limousine then pulled into the lot and eased its way up to the church entrance. The driver—someone unfamiliar—jumped out and opened the back door. Vince was the first out, followed by Marnie and Vince's kids, Michael, Paul, and Vickie, whom I recognized from her photo. They went into the church while the driver got back behind the wheel and looked for the best place to park where it wouldn't be in the way.

A silver Lexus was next to pull into the church lot and, once it was parked, Wyatt Worsley got out. Unaware he was being watched, he pulled a piece of paper from his pocket and looked at it, and then glanced up at the church. Deciding he was at the right place, he went inside.

A few other people I did not recognize, but assumed were connected with the church itself and not official mourners, entered. Finally a vintage yellow Ford Thunderbird pulled in, spluttering like Jack Benny's Maxwell, and parked in the first empty spot before seemingly dying. Evan Sandburg got out. He was dressed in a plain dark blue suit, though his hair and sunglasses were still Kingly.

Hannah and I were the last to go into the church.

The interior was relatively simple and modern-looking, not at all neo-Gothic. An organ was softly playing, and the open coffin was in front of the altar. Vince and his family were stationed in front of it, and Sandburg walked up to pay his respects, but Worsley remained seated in a pew.

"I'd prefer not going up," Hannah whispered to me.

"You don't have to," I said. But I went. I had never actually seen Annemarie Mazetta, the person who had been complicating my life for the past week.

On the way up I passed Vince and shook his hand, then went to the coffin.

Even though the funeral brochure put Annemarie's age at forty-eight, her dead face looked younger. Maybe it was the mortician's skill, or maybe she had somehow managed to defy the effects of the hard living and drugs. Some people were lucky like that. She was laid out in a high-collared dress, presumably to cover any residual marks from her strangling.

"I'm sure if Philly were here, he'd be very sorry," I whispered to her.

She didn't react.

After I returned to my pew, the priest stepped forward to begin the funeral mass. It was quickly evident he really had no idea who Annemarie Mazetta was, but he did the best he could with such generalities as she was taken far too soon, even God was angry about her senseless murdered, and so on.

Once he had concluded the scripted parts, he called for anyone who so wished to come up and speak about Annemarie.

This was the part of the service I was both prepared for and, in a way, dreading.

You'd better be right, a voice said inside my head.

It was Dane Colfax.

Vince was the first to get up and speak. He focused on Annemarie's good qualities, most of which emerged when she was young, and finished with the heartbreakingly sincere wish that he had done more to help her. Marnie comforted him when he returned to his pew.

Next up were Paul and Vickie, both of whom talked (rather unemotion-ally) about Annemarie as a mother and, how even in those times when she was struggling most desperately with her problems, she still loved them.

I hoped it was true.

Surprisingly, the next person to stand before the non-crowd was Evan Sandburg, who said he would say goodbye the best way he knew how, and then launched into an a cappella rendition of *Are You Lonesome Tonight?*

As Elvis clones go, his voice was as good as his appearance and, by the bridge, the organist had managed to join in. It appeared to be making Wyatt Worsley squirm, though.

At the end of his song, Sandburg pulled out a scarf and gently laid it on Annemarie's body. I doubted the scarf would be buried with her.

Once the King had returned to his seat (to a smattering of applause), the priest came forward and said, "Is there anyone else?"

Clearly he was hoping to end the service and move on to whatever else he had scheduled that day.

I was about to disappoint him.

Walking to the front, I said, "For those of you who don't know me, I'm Dave Beauchamp, and I work as a private investigator. I must say this has been a beautiful service. I've enjoyed it."

A small gasp arose.

"Um, no, I didn't really mean I *enjoyed* it in the sense that I had fun in the presence of someone who's dead, what I mean was…um…"

Dig a little deeper, the voice of Peter Lorre prodded. *You can still see the sun.*

"It was a beautiful ceremony," I reiterated. "You might be asking why I'm up here, since I didn't know Annemarie Mazetta. In fact, before today, I never met her. I mean, she's dead, so I can't really say I met her at all."

"We get it, Beauchamp," Vince called. "What is it you're trying to say?"

"Right, okay. What I'm trying to say is…I never met Annemarie, but I did meet her killer."

Now the gasp was bigger.

"Vince, I'm really sorry to tell you this, but there's no question that Philly killed Annemarie."

Vince stood up, though it was hard to tell. "You're crazy!" he shouted.

I shook my head and said, "Not this time. His fingerprints were found on the bracelet she was wearing when she died. He choked her with the handles of a cloth grocery bag that he'd earlier used to carry ears of corn home from the store. Traces of cloth and corn silk were found on her body."

"Jesus Christ," Vince muttered, then quickly crossed himself. "Why would Philly do such a thing?"

"I'm not completely sure yet," I confessed, "but I think it was to protect you."

"Protect me? From what?"

"From whoever was sending those threatening letters. Please, Vince, just hear me out."

The pet food magnate sunk back down onto the pew and the priest checked his watch.

"I'll try to be brief, father," I said. "I used to be a lawyer, so what else could I be?"

The sound of crickets came back at me.

This Hercule Poirot routine was harder than it looked when Peter Ustinov did it.

"Right. Okay. For those who never knew Philly Lepkowitz, trust me when I say he was not the premeditated-killer type. Yet he did take Annemarie's life, almost certainly in the heat of anger, since Philly didn't know his own strength. The question now remains, who killed Philly? He was shot to death inside my office. Why he was there started as a mystery, but I now believe he went there to meet someone."

Paul Mazetta rose from his pew. "Excuse me, Mr. Beauchamp," he said, "but is all of this stuff you're saying true, or are you trying to pitch a movie script?"

"It is true," I replied. "Please bear with me."

"Because when people find out what I do, they sometimes try to sell me their stories."

"I am not doing that. I understand this is highly unusual—"

"*Highly*," the priest repeated pointedly.

"But I wanted to take advantage of the fact that everyone is here. Now, if I may continue?"

Paul sat back down.

"Thank you. At first I theorized that Philly's murderer called him, pretending to be me, and asked him to come to my office, but I no longer believe that. It does not fit the facts. Philly's killer didn't know where my office was located, which is why he had to write it down on a piece of lined notebook paper. This piece of paper, in fact."

From my pocket, I pulled the now-crumpled slip containing my address.

"I found this in my office building. The killer either dropped it or tried to throw it in the trashcan and missed. On the back of this paper, in the same handwriting, is a strange, coded message: *5/12–SNA TC G19, 10:40a.* It made absolutely no sense at first, until I learned what it meant. Five-twelve was a date, SNA is location code for John Wayne Airport in Orange County, TC is Terminal C, and G-nineteen is the gate number. 'Ten-forty a' is, obviously, the time of day. So it was a message reminding someone when and where to pick up an airline passenger. My first thought was that the flier was an out-of-town hit man who had been hired to kill Vince, but that did not explain who was there to pick him up."

"Daddy, why would someone want to kill you?" Vickie Mazetta asked.

"Let's listen to what the guy has to say, honey," he replied, apparently having decided I wasn't crazy after all.

"Which brings us to the next clue," I went on. "This one I discovered in my office after Philly's body was taken away. He had been seated at my desk when he was shot. At some point, probably when he realized that he was in mortal danger, he took a pencil and wrote something on the bottom of my desk drawer. He wrote the identity of his killer."

"Too cliché!" Paul shouted.

"Pauly, the mook's got the stage, let him talk," Vince said.

"Paul is right, Vince," I said. "It is a cliché. And here's another one. Philly's killer is in this room."

That resulted in the biggest gasp of all.

"Sorry, I should have said that right up front. Anyway, to make a long story short..."

"That would be a blessing from God," the priest interrupted.

"Um, right. So what Philly scrawled onto the bottom of my drawer were the initials WW."

After a second's pause, Wyatt Worsley leapt up off the pew. "Now just one minute, sir!" he shouted. "I'll have you know I was interrogated by the police and completely cleared of involvement. I have iron clad alibis for both murders. The detectives are satisfied I had nothing to do with any of this carnage!"

"And so am I, Mr. Worsley," I told him. "At first, though, you were my prime suspect. I'm the one who led the police to you, and I apologize for your inconvenience. My mind changed when I realized the position Philly would have been in when he wrote those letters. They would have been right-side-up the way he was sitting. But when I saw them, under my desk, from my perspective they were upside down. So he didn't really write WW. He really wrote—"

Marnie Mazetta leapt to her feet. "Now what are you saying?" she cried. "That Philly really wrote MM? Are you accusing me of killing him?"

"No, Marnie, I'm not. I might have considered you if the only clue was those scrawled initials, but there's still this note with the airport pickup instructions. Once I learned Vickie was arriving in L.A. by train, I realized there was no reason for you to go to an airport to pick anyone up. But who would go to an airport to pick someone up? Maybe someone whose job it was to rent limousines, someone whose initials are also MM."

Now Michael Mazetta jumped up, but he did not waste time protesting. Instead he ran up the aisle for the door, only to be stopped by Detective Colfax and two plainclothes officers standing unobserved in the back.

"Let me go!" Michael shouted.

While that was going on, Vince once more rose to his feet. "Beauchamp, I was wrong about you being crazy," he shouted. "Crazy's too mild a word. You're a psychopath! You need to be locked up!"

"I'm sorry, Vince, I really am. But Michael's trying to run out of here smacks of a confession."

Vince slid out of the pew and walked slowly up the aisle to his eldest son, who was now cuffed and being held by the police. "Tell me he's nuts, Mikey," he said. "Please tell me the guy's blown a fuckin' fuse."

He then crossed himself again.

Michael simply stared at him.

"Say something, Mike, for God's sake."

"He can't prove anything," the younger man said. Then looking at me he shouted, "You can't prove anything! And with my father's connections, you'd be a fool to try!"

"My connections to what?" Vince asked. "Mikey, what are you…oh, no."

"It's okay, Dad, I get it. Because we're in a church and a priest is here, you're playing innocent."

"Oh, Jesus Christ," Vince muttered, this time not bothering to cross himself.

"You really accepted your father's act, didn't you, Michael?" I called back. "It's a good act, but your dad is not really part of the Mafia. He doesn't make people swim with the fishes."

Michael Mazetta looked confused. Then Vince nodded in assent. "I had no idea you bought into all this, Mikey," he uttered.

I continued. "I'm sorry, Vince, but I'm willing to wager Michael is the one who sent you that image of the fish, the Mafia warning, because he thought it would strike terror into you."

"I need to sit down," Michael moaned, and Colfax let him. "You're really not a made man?" he asked his father.

"I'm really not, Mikey," Vince said. "Paul and Vickie, they know that."

"He's right, Mike," Vickie said. "I caught on a long time ago."

"We just play along," Paul added. "There's a producer in town who does the same exact thing. What made you think Dad was a real gangster?"

"Maybe it was good for Michael's business," I guessed. "Maybe telling everybody you're the scion of a mob boss made it easier to run your limo company, because it made everybody treat you with respect. Big cars have big trunks, after all."

"Respect," Michael said. "Respect. Power. Control. All the things I never had as a kid, particularly after you two came along." He glared up at his siblings.

"What did we do to hurt you?" Vickie asked plaintively.

"You existed. You had a mother. Mine died, remember? You had a father who paid attention to you."

"Of course I paid attention," Vince moaned. "They were babies, for Christ's sake! You take care of babies. The older kids can start to take care of themselves. I promise you, Mikey, Pauly and Vickie learned to take care of themselves earlier than I wanted."

Michael Mazetta leveled his defeated glare at me. "You still have no proof," he muttered.

I held up the note again. "I think once a handwriting expert compares the notations on this paper to the signatures in the service guest book, they'll find only one example that matches."

"Michael Mazetta," Colfax began, "I'm arresting you on suspicion of murder. You have the right to remain si—"

"I've been silent my whole miserable life!" Michael screamed.

Vince regarded him with red, moist eyes. "Mikey, yes or no," he said softly. "Did you kill Philly?"

Regarding his father with dry, cold eyes, Michael Mazetta replied, "Of course I did."

"*Why*, for God's sake?"

"Because he was a problem. The job of a boss is to eliminate problems. I *used* to think you knew that."

The priest stepped forward and asked, "Do you want to confess your sin, my son?"

"Thank you, Padre," Colfax responded for him, "but I think any further confession needs to be done at police headquarters."

"I'm so terribly sorry about all of this," the priest said, "but I am going to have to ask all of you to leave. We do need the church for an event this afternoon."

Worsley didn't need to be told twice, and left without saying a word or even nodding in acknowledgement.

Sandburg, though, stopped and said, "So, what did you think?"

"About the confession?" I asked.

"No, about the song. I sound like the real thing, don't I?"

"Yes, Evan, you do."

"This might be a whole new avenue of performing for me. I never even thought about funerals before, I can see it…let the King transport you to Heaven."

The last part was delivered in Elvisese.

I was about to suggest that for cremations he could sing *Burning Love*, but I managed to stop myself.

Once the King had gone, Vince came up and asked me to accompany the family to the cemetery for the burial, and I agreed. It seemed the least I could do.

Hannah opted to return home, and as she was hugging me goodbye said, "I know you wanted me to watch other people, but I couldn't take my eyes off of you. You looked like Nick Charles up there."

"How do you know Nick Charles?"

"Well, a few days ago when you were out, I was kind of bored and found a disc labeled *The Thin Man*. I thought it was an exercise video, so I put it in. Even though it wasn't what I was expecting, I watched it and kind of liked it, especially the end when they're just about to start doing it on the train. I didn't think you could go there in old movies."

When we had more time, I'd fill her in about pre-code Hollywood.

The Mazetta clan and I rode to Westwood Memorial Park in the stretch limo, and I figured we'd be returning to the church the same way. En route I said, "Vince, are you going to be all right?"

"Yeah," he wheezed. "But goddamn, I…I don't even know what to think. Was I really that lousy a father?"

"You're a great father, Dad," Paul said.

"This wouldn't have happened if I hadn't pretended I was a wise guy. I'm as guilty as he is."

"Daddy," Vickie said, "I got this creep at college to leave me alone by telling him that I was the real-life equivalent of Meadow Soprano. If you're guilty, then so are we."

"None of us is guilty of anything," Paul said. "Michael is just…"

"Conflicted," Vickie finished for him.

"How did you conclude that it was Michael who was behind all this?" Marnie asked me.

Did I mention she was wearing the Kim Novak black dress from *Vertigo*?

"Would you believe me if I said the final epiphany came from the thought of a picture hanging upside down?"

"At this point, I'd believe anything."

"Dammit, Philly…" Vince said, starting to cry. Marnie put an arm around him, and his kids laid a supportive hand on each leg.

"Was Michael also behind those threatening letters?" Marnie asked.

"I'm sure he was, though I can't explain his motivation. It will come out. But once I decided Michael was involved, it answered another big question: *who* was following Vince. Michael found out from Philly where he was hiding, drove to the motel in Mission Hills, waited for Vince to leave, saw him get into the rental car, and then followed him back to my house. If I'm right, it means Michael took a shot at me while I was driving Vince's rental car under the assumption that I was Vince. I don't believe he wanted to kill you, Vince. I think it was a further attempt to frighten you.

Vince managed to compose himself by the time we got to Wilshire Boulevard, from which one accessed Westwood Memorial Park…if one knew how. The cemetery was literally one of the most historic, best-kept secrets in Los Angeles, renowned for being the final resting place of Marilyn Monroe, yet virtually hidden from the major thoroughfare fronting it.

"Why, Beauchamp?" Vince asked as the limo squeezed in through the entrance. "What the holy hell was this whole damn thing about anyway?"

"Vince, that I don't know," I replied. "But I promise you I'll find out."

After the ceremony at the grave site Vince and his family were ready to get back in the limo, but I asked for a few more minutes.

"Why?" Vince asked. "What's so important we have to stay here?"

"I need to find my sister," I told him. "I just want to say hello."

TWENTY ONE

If you've been following the news, you probably already know the rest of the story. Not surprisingly, this entire mess of a case was all about money.

Michael Mazetta's limo business may have been successful on the surface, but just underneath he was dealing with a series of financial setbacks: a lawsuit over an accident with one of his cars; a lawsuit over failure to pay alimony; and a few very bad nights at the Commerce Casino. In short, Michael was desperate for money.

He knew he could not rely on a loan from his father, since he had never paid back the one that enabled him to launch a business—except for the "gift" of Vince's limo—so he settled on the time-honored tool of extortion. The problem was he didn't know how to go about it.

Enter Annemarie.

Shortly after leaving Start Over Clinic she contacted Michael asking to borrow money, since the payoff that she had been expecting from Vince as incentive for completing rehab had been torpedoed by her being thrown out. While Michael didn't have the money, he took her into his house, and it took practically no time for the two to fall into bed.

Or *back* into bed since they had enjoyed a fling when Michael was still in high school.

Annemarie was more than willing to help Michael take Vince to the cleaners so the two of them concocted a plot to threaten and ultimately kidnap him and hold him for ransom. The letters—which were unlovingly composed by Annemarie—were to announce the plan and the fish picture was to be the final step to frighten him. Annemarie fed Michael's belief that his father was a big man with the mob by filling him with imaginary anecdotes of her ex's Mafia activities.

There were two things on which they did not count: Vince's decision to disappear before they could kidnap him, and Philly's loyalty.

I now realize that Michael's phone call to me asking if I knew Vince's whereabouts did not come from a standpoint of filial concern. He was literally trying to track Vince down so he could make him disappear again. I also realized the woman's voice I heard in the background must have been Annemarie. That was the only contact I had with her while she was alive.

It was also Annemarie who discovered the depth of Philly's devotion to his boss...the hard way.

Growing increasingly anxious and irritated that the kidnap and extortion scheme had hit a roadblock, Annemarie made a serious mistake: she called Vince's house. Marnie was not there at the time, but Philly was, and it was he who took her call. What exactly was said will never be known, but based on the details of Michael's confession, Philly had demanded that Annemarie stop bothering Vince, which inflamed her already unstable psyche so much that she blurted out the extortion plan.

Attempting to prove to Philly that she was in complete control of the situation, she presented the scheme as entirely her own, never mentioning Michael's involvement—an act of hubris that sealed her fate.

Despite the fact that Philly Lepkowitz lacked formal education and had a propensity to mangle the English language, he was not an idiot. He sensed Annemarie had lost her grip on reality, particularly when she claimed she'd send Elvis Presley to kill Vince if he didn't pony up the money. Ever-loyal Philly made her a counter-offer: *he* would give her $20,000 of his own money if she would promise to leave Vince alone forever. Desperate for money—and realizing she could cut Michael out of this deal and keep every penny for herself—she agreed, telling Philly to meet her under the Malibu Pier after dark, with the cash.

Whether or not it was a serious error in judgment for Annemarie to take one of Michael's town cars to the rendezvous without his knowledge, let alone permission, is a matter that is open for interpretation. Had she not, she would likely still be dead, but Philly might still be alive and Michael would not be sitting in jail right now with his father unwilling to post bail. But she did take the car, which Michael saw, and he decided to follow her in his Beemer. He didn't even need to follow closely since he had GPS trackers installed in all of his cars and limos, protection against attempted theft.

Michael tailed her all the way to Malibu just to see what she was up to. From a distance he watched as she waited under the pier. When it became dusky, he was able to creep a little closer and still remain unseen.

Before long Philly, whom Michael recognized, arrived carrying the cloth grocery bag filled with money. Upon moving closer Michael was able to hear their conversation, largely because Annemarie's voice was very loud when she was high, and Philly's was not dulcet at the best of times.

That was when Annemarie made the biggest mistake of her soon-to-be-extinguished life.

She started laughing at Philly and telling him he was a "pussy boy" who went down on her ex-husband whenever he was told. She asked Philly if he used Vince as a sex toy and laughed even more maniacally.

When Philly angrily grabbed her by the arms and shook her, she shrieked, "Rape!"

Philly tried to shut her up, but she screamed even louder and (according to Michael's statement) cackled in between each scream.

Blinded by rage, Philly took the cash-laden grocery bag, shoved the straps over her head to her neck, and then twisted them.

This part didn't appear in the news coverage: Michael told Colfax it only took twenty seconds for Annemarie to have the life squeezed out of her.

Suddenly realizing what he'd done, Philly cried, "Aw, no!" and started to run.

He returned to scoop up the part of the $20,000 that had fallen onto the sand, and put it back in the bag. Then he fled.

Michael had seen everything.

A few people appeared, responding to the screams. Michael told them he was simply filming a movie, and not to worry. When asked by a beach-comber where the film equipment was, he held up his smartphone.

"These days you can make a movie with one of these," he told the people.

Michael then jumped in his Beemer and took off, leaving the town car Annemarie had borrowed where it was. He arranged for it to be retrieved the next day, after her body had been discovered.

Now Michael was operating on his own and afraid the entire plan was fated to go belly-up.

He called my phone pretending to be his father, and doing Vince's voice convincingly, in hopes of throwing me off the track through the implication that Vince was already being held by someone. Then he called Philly and pulled the same trick, pretending once more to be Vince. Michael asked Philly to meet him and Philly agreed to do so in my office, giving Michael the address. He scrawled it on that same slip of paper containing information for a totally unrelated airport pickup.

I would love to know why Philly chose my office for the meeting, going so far as to let himself in with a lock pick before Michael got there... but there is no one to ask.

When Michael finally arrived, he found Philly seated behind my desk. He told Philly that he had witnessed the murder of Annemarie and would turn him over to the police unless two conditions were met. One was money...$50,000 this time...and the other that he tell Michael where Vince was.

Philly proved willing to talk about what transpired between him and Annemarie, but refused to reveal that he knew where Vince was hiding out...at least until Michael pulled a gun on him. With an automatic trained on his heart, Philly was instructed to place his own gun on the desk, which

Michael then picked up.

The venerable phrase "You'll have to kill me first!" is far more potent in the abstract than when you have two loaded guns pointed at your chest, which is why Philly finally revealed that Vince was hiding in the motel in Mission Hills. Since from Michael's standpoint Philly was no longer needed, he shot him with his own gun and left the big guy in my office.

What Michael did not know, of course, was that Philly was busy scrawling his initials under my desk while he was being held at gunpoint.

I'd say *that* just about wrapped things up, but there remained a few unanswered questions which were not vital to the outcome of the case, but were loose ends nonetheless.

The answer to one of them—the seeming coincidence of Annemarie choosing my father's law firm to represent her against the Start Over Clinic—was revealed when it was learned Annemarie had befriended Laurie Lomax, another woman at the clinic, who happened to be the daughter of Darrell Lomax, a senior partner in Allen, Garbedian and Lomax. It was Laurie who recommended her daddy's firm to Annemarie should she ever want to file suit.

The second question was answered when I went to my office at the end of the month to start packing things up in order to move out.

Going through my desk drawer, I found a folded piece of paper that I did not recognize. Opening it, I found a letter written in pencil:

Dear Mr. B,

I hope you dont mind my using your office. I let myself in. Dont ask me how. Youd probly get mad knowing. Somebody called me claiming to be Mr. M, but I knew it wasnt really him. He kept talking like he was the capo in a gangster movie, which the boss never would have done, not around me, anyway. But I played along and when the guy said he wanted to meet me I suggested your office. I didnt know what was about to happen so I sure didn't want to put Mrs. M at risk at home, and I wasnt about to invite the guy to my place. Nobody comes to my place. My place is only for me. So I pertended I had an office, and the only actual office I know of is yours. I sure hope you don't mind.

Whoever this bozo is, I want to find out why he was pertending to be the boss, who is really sitting in a motel a ways up the freeway.

If anything happens to your office I appologize in advance, and I'll make it up to you later.

Yrs.

Philly

P.S.: Your a real mensch and Mr. M likes you, even though he growls.

I read the note again and suddenly had the strangest craving for a *catchapino*. It was hard to tell if Philly liked apostrophes or not since he clearly never met one. I don't know if I could have prevented Philly's murder had I been there, but I would have gone down trying.

EPILOGUE

What more can there be to say?

How about the wedding is back on?

Richard Neale called us into his office not only to discuss some estate matters, but more importantly, tell us that the case against Hannah brought by what was left of the Temple of Theotologics had been thrown out of court. The judge had been swayed by the number of testimonials Neale had gathered stating that Palmer Hanley was in perfect mental health right up to the moment of his murder. Dick had also provided a copy of the tape Palmer had made as a prelude to writing his autobiography, in which he revealed, in detail, the workings of the Temple and how he was treated during his captivity.

But what really caused the suit to bounce out of the court like Thor's hammer on a trampoline was the fact that the judge had a niece who had fallen victim to the Temple, and he was having none of its argument.

Dick also recommended a friend of his who worked as a wealth management planner, and his investment efforts have already resulted in sizeable returns on our inheritances. Unless the Martians land and wreck everything, we're pretty much set.

Despite all that, Hannah and I have still not set the date. I am waiting for Dad to recover a little more so he can act as my best man.

It shouldn't be much longer.

Mom tries to act casual but Dad's heart attack shook her to her core. She still snipes at him occasionally, but now does it with a smile. How their relationship will change and what happens with Colleen will have to play out on its own. Having finally been declared an adult, I'm doing the adult thing and staying out of it.

I've seen Vince once since the day of the funeral. I offered to give back the remainder of the thousand dollars he gave me, but he waved it away, saying, "You nearly took a bullet for me, so keep it." Privately Marnie told me he'd been severely depressed by the entire situation, though after Michael opted for a guilty plea, sparing a trial and more bad press for the family, Vince relented and paid for an attorney to represent him in the sentencing phase. Michael got twenty-five to life.

Of late, every time I look at my painting of the unknown, solitary man walking down a rainy street I think instead of the man I'll never know that

Michael picked up from John Wayne airport. Whoever he is at this moment is walking down his own personal street, completely unaware he'd been driven by a murderer.

"The King" has found a new regular gig, doing weekend shows at Hollywood Everlasting Memorial Park, the resting place of the stars.

Dead celebrities will never again be "lonesome tonight."

Even though my office is shuttered, Hannah and I are still in the apartment. It's not a case of sentiment; we just haven't found the perfect house yet.

When the phone rang one afternoon I thought it might be a realtor calling with a new lead. When the caller identified himself, though, Hannah saw my shocked expression and nervously asked, "Who is it?"

Holding the phone down I said, "It's your brother Christian. He wants to talk with you."

Hannah hesitated for several seconds before taking the receiver.

"Hi, Chris."

There was a long silence before she spoke again.

"Yes, what you heard is true. I am worth millions. No, I am *not* using drugs. I don't do that anymore. Yes, I have plans for the money. What?" After another pause she held the phone down and said, "He wants me to make a big cash donation to his campaign. What should I say?"

"It's your money, Hannah," I told her. "But if you do give it to him, he'll never go away. He'll be back for more, and more after that."

Putting the phone back to her ear, Hannah said, "Chris, I'll tell you what. I never cashed that five-thousand-dollar check. I'll send it back to you as my donation. What? *How much?*"

To me she said, "I can't believe it! He's asking for a hundred-thousand dollars!"

After a second, Hannah went back on the phone. "Christian, you're my brother, and part of me will always love you, but...*go swim with the fishes!*"

She dropped the receiver in the cradle.

Couldn't have put it better myself! the voice of Marlon Brando said inside my head.

ABOUT THE AUTHOR

Michael Mallory is the author of the *Amelia Watson* historical mystery series, the *Dave Beauchamp* Hollywood mystery series (published by Wildside Press), and the standalone novels *The Mural* (also published by Wildside) and *Death Walks Skid Row*. His short stories—some 140 to date—have been published in major magazines and anthologies. A recognized authority on film and animation history, he has also written eleven books on pop culture subjects and more than 600 magazine and newspaper articles. A former radio newscaster and television actor, Mike lives in the Los Angeles area.

www.ingramcontent.com/pod-product-compliance
Lightning Source LLC
Chambersburg PA
CBHW050753250626
47155CB00005B/2041